ONE HORSE TOWN

G.A. SMITH

LONGSAINTS PRESS

·   ·   ·   ·   ·

Print, eBook and Cover by
N.D. Author Services [NDAS]
www.NDAuthorServices.com

"Aspen Grove"
cover art by
Pete Anderson

Just a sec.
I forgot to tell you something before you go.

TABLE OF CONTENTS

CHAPTER ONE:
GRAMMAR

You don't know me at all and that's okay as far as we are right now, and so I hope you don't mind if I just say some very obvious things, and whether they are to you or not that's okay too.

I just wanted to say something about grammar, just in case you didn't know. You only ever get three tenses, right? There's just past and present and hopefully future, right? There are some others that none of us ever bother understanding, so let's just end with that, because that's all you ever really get in this life and I suppose that's fine with pretty much everyone on a regular basis. The only thing I want to say here about that is I don't quite follow those things anymore like I used to: past, present and maybe future. I want to tell you something but I can't say how it's going to go. I have this feeling I'm going to be mixing up my tenses such as they are, were, might be.

If I was in past tense, then that's kind of difficult to say. That's only partially because of problems with memory. There was the mass shooting at my little college, and Larry my best friend was in the room next door when the killer came in, and there were many dead and some I cannot see because I can't anymore and Larry and I are fishing, and he is telling me where to stand in the river because he's been a steelhead guide on this river for years and years and now he is teaching college classes and then we are in the office talking and then there is a woman on the ground and I cannot see her any longer to describe what the killer has done because I see her head and body and I can't see that anymore and there is no sense in description and that is past I think and Larry is saying something about red dragonflies which is past and present and future because I am seeing it all at once just shattered and I am running away from the shooter, the killer, and Larry is in the same room with him, and so many others, and it is October First in one year or another and I don't think it was very long ago but time is broken.

There is something else there that if I could just get at it then I would be fine or maybe not and it's hard to remember anymore. I remember fishing. I think I want to remember the fishing, but even that won't leave me alone.

Once, when I was fishing, after having scrabbled down the shale-slide bank in the heat of late summer and found myself before the river where I intended to fish, I cast my fly line for some little bit, and it was so very hot that morning that I had no waders on and just waded in the cool snow-melt water in my jeans and shoes.

And then there was a rustling in the dry grass and sage-scrub and tiny Russian Willows behind me, a sound unnatural in some way that I didn't know, like those other sounds somewhere in the past or future, the gunshots that I didn't know were gunshots at first, just dull thuds against the wall separating my classroom from his, and I turned and saw a rattlesnake, many feet long, as thick as a large man's arm, reach into a tree and grab a robin. There was no thinking then, just something entirely primal happening, and I jumped into the river and swam across to the other side and stood there, just feeling the breath coming out of my lungs again and again, and I never went back there ever.

When I heard those shots in the room next door and finally understood what they meant because those sounds had no place in that place I just yelled at my students to get out and ran. That's all I could do. That's all there is to say, and I couldn't go back there again either. I had to go away, you see? Leave past present and future. I had to.

There is something else here in this past or present or future tense that I want to talk about and it just nags and gnaws at me like an animal on my arm or ankle or leg or mind or maybe it is just something saying something in my ears, but I cannot think about it, because it is hidden from me now and I have a hard time identifying what it is. I hope it is just fishing. I want that to be all it is.

If I am in the present tense then the present tense is Dobbins, Montana, a little town up by the Rockies and a little house where my wife Joanie and I live with our three dogs. It's where we, or maybe more to the truth, where I ran away to after the shooting. I kind of work for the local paper here, writing a column each week. I have a pickup truck named Chuck whom everyone knows, but that's another story. I sometimes get confused about things, or maybe I just don't care like I used to or maybe it's because I don't remember how to care, and a doctor once told me that was an effect of PTSD but I'm not so sure about that because people have told me all kinds of things about what's happened to me and I just don't know. I try to go fishing as often as I can in the summer and survive Montana winters. That's about it.

It's the future tense I worry about. Sometimes the past and present seem to make a mess of what might be the future, or maybe it's because I seem to keep screwing things up in the present that muddies the waters. I used to have a pretty good idea of the future as far as anyone can say they have, but I've come to learn that futures can end as quickly as the pulling of a trigger and so I worry about it. I can't help it.

Past present future.

Chapter Two:
The Great Hay Bale Heresy

There has always been a great deal of controversy in this world of ours. It has caused wars and revolutions and countless deaths and recriminations, deportations and reservations and so much harm that one cannot fathom it all. When the various sides battle in these arguments, the winners write the history and tell their own tales, and that's the way it's always been.

I try not to watch the news any longer because that just sort of seems like the safe thing to do if you want to stay on an even keel with the real world that you interact with each day. and here in our parcel of Montana I don't much care what's out there anymore, but every so often I figure what the heck, I wonder if there's anything going on out there that might warrant my attention? Unfortunately, that's when I find out people are upset about just the craziest of things and I think maybe they should just move to a tiny town in Montana where none of that matters and you'd find out pretty quickly how it didn't matter, because all you want to do here is survive winter and live like mad during the summer.

However, here in our little corner of the enormous state of Montana one is not safe from controversy as well, and so if you thought that you could escape that kind of thing, then you will unfortunately come to find out otherwise. The problem here, which I have grown to understand, and is something on the order of a matter of internecine conflict based on deep religious faith, is hay bales.

Now, I know what you're thinking: how in the world could a hay bale bother anyone? I mean, what sort of objections might there be given a configuration of grasses, and how might anyone find offense in such a case? In order to explain this, I will need to take you deep inside the secret conclaves of the faithful.

If you're like me, and of course I don't know you at all but I'm just saying you know, then you don't want any sort of digressions in a story because you just want to go ahead and get on with it. So, I'm sorry about that, but in order to explain the import of this particular controversy it's necessary that I first explain the importance of grass. Oh, I know, you're already unhappy about that, but the reason you are is because grass is one of those things that you have taken for granted all your life, and you really ought to stop doing that if you get the chance.

So, first things first, grass is God's Number One Thing. It's the most pervasive and successful plant on this planet of ours, and it comes in perhaps something on the order of a ka-jillion varieties, and I'm not kidding about that. Grass is like gravity: it's the thing that holds all of everything else in place, and keeps it from crumbling away under our feet and blowing away into space. You're thinking I'm exaggerating I know, but here in our own little country, back in the 1930's, we managed the greatest ecological disaster of all time just by plowing under the grass. Go ahead and look it up when you've got a minute. No, you have to understand, grass is everything.

Here in the expanses around Dobbins, grass is life. It is precious. People have gone to prison and lost their lives over it. Grass is everything and I'm not fooling. Grass is the life-blood of every rancher in the state, and the water that grows it of course. When you have two-and-a-half months of growing season to collect all the hay you possibly can to keep your herd alive for the next nine-and-a-half months, yes, grass is life. It's the only thing that's keeping you on your place, because without it, your herd starves and then so do you. Got it?

But, the kicker is, water is even more precious than that, because no water and then no grass and that's when the shooting starts. In our parcel of this very large world we have been blessed with running rivers and the snowmelt to keep them alive all summer long. This is not the case elsewhere in the state or country, but here God has blessed us with all the water we might need, and so also all the grass one might ever wish for. That's why the Church of Hay Bales grew up here in the first place, and thus allowed for the later Great Schism. I am sorry to say that I had something to do with that, well, maybe.

Okay, let me just get you caught up on the particular religious factions here, and then maybe you can understand a bit better what's going on and why I have been branded an agnostic and apparently a heathen as well in some quarters. So, here's the thing: we have two Churches, the Church of The Round Balers and The Church of The Square Balers.

Now you have to understand that labels are of course always deceptive, and tend to be applied by those outside the faith. I mean, "square bales" are not square at all, they're truly rectangular of course, and then the "round bales", well, that's sort of silly because they actually are more like gigantic Twinkies than anything else.

If I understand correctly, and I don't, because parishioners of both Churches tell a different story, at one point there was only One Church and it was the Church of Square Bales, or maybe it was Round Bales, but that's where the heresy or maybe blasphemy or at least something enters into it. The way the story goes is that it was all one way or the other, and then this fellow from all the way over in Missoula shows up and he's a farm equipment salesman and he's obviously proselytizing and trying to convert folks to his own Church. Anyway, whichever way it goes, he comes in and convinces *somebody* to get a "different" baler and that's when the bales hit the fan if you know what I mean.

My own experience is that faith is very different for all of us. I mean, you can be an absolutely spiritual person and be okay with God even if you can't make the drive on Sunday, so there's no way I'm going to be judgmental about how one approaches The Almighty.

For the Round Balers, life is an aesthetic thing in which all of God's Creation is a reverence to it. You have to just imagine round bales, sitting in a gigantic landscape, and you'd know immediately what I mean. They are pastoral, bucolic, the thing you'd stop and take a picture of and say ahhh, this is real life, the real thing. Round bales exist I believe so that folk artists can paint those kind of squarish-looking cows standing next to them in perfect bliss. They are something a Giant steps down out of the Rockies to place each morning into his cereal bowl. They are soft. They have no sharp edges. They are round. They are the places of dalliance in those romance novels. You want to just sleep next to the darn things.

Then of course there are square bales, which reflect the grand symmetry and purpose of the universe, the great connectedness of things. They are emblems of God's Plan for things and our place in it all. They are the Rules which we all live by and find our way. They are efficient and necessary, and exude a strong sense of work ethic. They tell us what is necessary in this life. And besides, how do you stack round bales? That's absurd! If everything was round then there'd be no progress at all, everything would just be rolling around willy-nilly and nothing would get done! Square bales lie on the ground as they're supposed to until needed, and very large adolescents chuck them into trucks for their summer income. They're good for everyone. I've met some of these adolescents and most of them are going to play college football in the fall and so that has to be a good thing, right? And how in the world can you make a pyramid out of round bales if you wanted to and astound and impress tourists, such as they are? Or a good Halloween maze, huh? No way you're doing that with those silly round bales.

Okay, here's the part I really don't want to talk about, because I, unwittingly, set off the Great Schism myself, or so it seems, or maybe just made it public, or maybe just rekindled an old feud. It was one of those, or maybe more than one I don't know. For my own part I will defend myself via the First Amendment and was simply saying my say, though I admit, rather publically, which is probably never a good idea.

The deal here is that the two greatest Bishops of Bale in our county are Einar Einarson and Jack Jackson, and to some degree both of them play a part in something later that I want to say but I can't just yet. Jack and Einar own pretty much everything you can see in our part of the world, if you get up on a step ladder or stand just-so on a mountain top, and when they have something to say about pretty much anything, folks listen. Now you already know that I don't actually know, but Jack is a Round Baler and Einar is a Square Baler, and each of them says that the other is a heretic and the Church was going fine until the other one got there with his bit of blasphemy. Fine, that's their problem. The real problem, however, is that I wrote a column about one of them, and their very fine hay bales.

So, I went out to Jack's place to interview him about some new cows he had, and no I can't remember their name, it starts with a "C" I think, as in "Cows", but anyway I'd heard he'd been in South America recently at a cattle convention and so that's what I came out to talk to him about because he had been a guest speaker there.

Jack is a bit of an anomaly around here for a variety of reasons. For one thing, Jack is African American, and in this part of Montana you can count African American ranchers on one finger, and before you start to get all indignant on me about bringing this up, I mention it solely because it's a factor in something else I want to tell you later, so bear with me. Another thing that stands out about Jack is that he is always impeccably dressed, even out in the middle of a herd of cattle. His cowboy boots are shiny and his Stetson is dapper. His jeans are always clean and even his chambray shirts appear to be pressed, and he wears a string tie whenever you see him. Jack has a herd of men at his beck and call of course, and I've never actually heard him raise his voice about anything. He's a gentleman, and gentlemen don't shout. When some shouting needs to be done he merely says something to someone who's always standing nearby and let's them do the shouting.

So, my interview with Jack was set up for one morning and Chuck and I headed out early to make the appointment. We drove through miles and miles of Jack's place on the way to his home, and the countryside was beautiful. Here and there streams meandered through green meadows and stands of pine and fir. Every so often you'd catch a glimpse of the big river that runs through his place, and everywhere you looked you saw the lovely round bales, dotting a mountain meadow like sprinkles on ice cream.

And so, when I pulled up to Jack's place and was ushered inside one of the first things I said by way of greeting was how nice Jack's hay bales were. Jack smiled at that and led me into his study where we sat down and before the interview even began he said, "Would you do me a small favor? When you write your column would you mind just mentioning somewhere in the article how very nice my hay bales are?" I said that of course I would, and Jack smiled, very pleased apparently.

I wrote that column as soon as I got home both because it was very interesting how someone from our neck of the woods actually rubbed elbows with ranchers from all over the world at international conferences and was a guest speaker to boot, but also because my list of people to interview was getting a bit thin. I mention this only to note that the column came out in The Paper the same Saturday after the interview, and also to make you aware of the fact that it was Saturday afternoon when I got a call from Einar Einarson.

I've met Einar before, just briefly down at Del's, but like Jack, everyone knows who he is. You don't own half the county without people knowing who you are.

I suppose that's why I was a bit surprised when he identified himself over the phone: "Hi Al, this is Einar. I just wanted to let you know that I've got something over here at the Bar-S-Bar that you might be interested in for your next column."

Naturally I said that I was and I asked what it might be, but Einar was a bit coy about saying anything more about it, so we set up a time for me to come out, and before he hung up all he said was "Oh, and bring a camera."

So, early one morning the following week Chuck and I set out for Einar's place, which was a good hour and a half drive over country roads, but I didn't mind the long drive because I was real curious what it was that he had going on that he wanted me to see. Chuck and I meandered through Einar's property for about forty-five minutes before we reached his home, much like we had when visiting Jack's place, and once again the countryside was simply stunning.

Einar's place also has a famous river that runs through it, and you can bet that when we're done talking I'm going to ask if he wouldn't mind if I fished a place I just saw a time or two, and the timber on his place is enormous, mostly Lodgepole and some firs, interwoven by streams from someone's imagining of a grand and manicured golf course, and ponds that perhaps Narcissus looked into, ringed with flowers. And yes, I also noticed Einar's hay bales, because you couldn't help but notice them. These were not those kinds of smallish affairs that you might see large people chucking into a truck, oh no. These were huge slabs of straw, no doubt shifted only by heavy machinery. They were massive and irresolute.

Einar was there in his bricked driveway when we pulled up to his place, and I couldn't help but think how odd such a driveway was out here in the middle of nowhere, but everyone has his tastes for things. Einar's home is a massive log affair, which didn't very much surprise me, given both Einar's heritage and his own stature. My own specialty as a professor was in Norse and Irish studies, and if you read Norse history and literature you run across all kinds of descriptions of very large men: Harald Hardrautha who invaded England in 1066, for example, who was supposed to be seven feet tall, and Rolf-the-Walker, who was said to be so large he couldn't ride a horse. Einar's got that blood, because he looks almost exactly like one of his hay bales: just utterly massive.

He was dressed in overalls and had a very nice flannel shirt on and for the life of me I can't imagine where he gets shirts that could possibly fit him. I imagine him at the Wal-Mart in Butte, going down the aisle: small, medium, large, Big and Tall, and then finally, at the very end he's able to come to the Mammoth section to see what the latest fashion is. Of course, given that this is Einar, I assume that in reality he has a tailor somewhere back East, who maybe has to do a bit of slumming with flannel because the money is good. If people were horses, Einar is a Clydesdale.

When Chuck pulled us into the drive and I got out, Einar was there with a big grin on his face and enveloped my puny hand with one of his own. Being in proximity to Einar like this I reconsidered that heavy machinery might not be actually necessary to move those bales, but then I remembered that there was only one Einar to cover ten thousand acres or so, so no, ordinary human beings probably needed machines for that.

"Al!" Einar boomed. "Hey, how's Chuck these days? Great of you to come all the way out here. I just wanted to show you a bit of something that I've been working on for a while. It's kind of one of those pet projects of a sort. Come on, we'll take my truck."

Oddly, this made me kind of nervous for some reason. You have to be inside my skin right now to understand because I'm kind of nervous about almost anything anymore, but you have to see my thinking just a bit: the two wealthiest and powerful individuals in the entire county, roughly the size of certain northeastern states, have just invited me to their homes.

Something wasn't quite right here, and Einar was being very close to the chest about what it was, but I looked back at Chuck for a second and then back at Einar and smiled and said "Okay."

We bounced along some dirt roads for a mile or two and then Einar pulled us into a little meadow ringed with pines and we got out. I was stunned. I stood and looked and that was all I could do. I made a few steps and stopped again. There in front of me was Stonehenge. Stonehenge made of hay bales. And no, not just some hay bales stacked up on end, but an honest-to-goodness replica of Stonehenge. The entire Giant's Dance, maybe even to scale.

I know what I'm talking about here. Every trilithon and lintel was in place just where it should be, and there was even a horizontal bale laid out like the Altar Stone. It was perfect. If you stood a distance from it you could imagine these were real stones and that you were really standing at Stonehenge, minus the crowds of tourists. It really was the Real Deal, and if you knew what you were seeing, you'd be transported to a time and place where everything was, well, where everything was different. A different world. I was amazed and said so. Einar smiled broadly.

"So, what do you think, huh? Not so bad, eh?"

"It's amazing, Einar. Just absolutely amazing."

And then Einar just beamed like the morning sun coming over a ridge and told me about how he had studied up on Stonehenge and had gotten a contractor to come out and do measurements and "Yep. It's completely to scale," and about how he'd done it all by himself on weekends. I was absolutely flabbergasted and must have taken three dozen photos in-between being awed by it all.

"Einar, I'm going to get this column out this Saturday. I can't wait to write this."

And I did, and when The Paper came out there were lots of calls and emails about the column, with people exclaiming about how very interesting that was, and ancient history comes to Dobbins, and of course there were a few about oh no, now we'll have those stupid Druid-people all over the place. Anyway. People really seemed to like that one for the most part, and of course I was gushing about it myself.

However, on Sunday afternoon while Joanie and I were sitting on the front porch with Grip and Tan, a brand-new Ford pickup came up the drive, and Joanie and I wondered who it could be. Out got Jack Jackson, and his expression was rather grim.

I kind of hate to just stop there, but it turns out this is a sort of complicated story and I have to tell you some other things to make sense of it all. Again, my apologies.

CHAPTER THREE:
THESE DAYS

We lost Finn this past winter, of our three dogs. We have, I need to say had, Grip and Tan and littlest Finn. He was somewhat smaller than the others and greater in heart. He was such a gentle soul. He was the best if I can say so of my own children without sounding as though I loved the others less. He went when he had to and we all hurt so very much. Grip and Tan lay down with him, Joanie and I sat, waiting, and when he passed they howled and howled, and we did too.

He burned like a bonfire all his life, and he must have known, maybe they all do, how fast their lives are, running and shouting and laughing at everything and running all their lives, just burning every moment of it all the time, even when they're sleeping. I wish I could live like that I think sometimes. I don't know how many days I have left, but they should all just be a-fire, don't you think?

We think about him all the time. Joanie hurts worse than me, because you see the dogs really are her children and she spends much of every day with them, and when Finn passed, her very favorite child, something changed, and I didn't see and I didn't understand

and there are times when you miss just a moment and then it's gone. And it's important. You miss just that little something and everything else depends on it. You have to be looking you know. You can't just be busted up yourself and be thinking just about yourself. You have to be looking. Looking out.

There are two bowls out for breakfast and dinner. Not three. There are two dogs in the back of the truck or car, not three. Whatever we do, it just chokes us up. It's hard. Harder on Joanie I think. I walked past her bedroom one night when I couldn't sleep and I heard her crying. I didn't go in. I don't even know what to do anymore. It hurts. It's hurt us.

If anyone asked me, and they never do, how things are going these days with me and Joanie I'd say "Okay" and know that I was lying. I don't know what I'm doing or not doing, but whatever it is or isn't, it's not good. I wish I was lying about that, but I don't think I am but sometimes I don't know. I want to know, but I don't know how to go about it. Maybe I can learn how to learn again?

These days there are days of silence. They are the days when there's anger about something, and it really doesn't matter what it is. There are the seasons and the snow and the blossoms and we're turning the new year, but we're not turning together like we used to. We used to turn, always, together, like the new leaves, the new grass, the first snow. Always together. Two halves of all things.

It's as if we don't want to any longer. Neither of us. Some line has been crossed that can't be clearly identified, and neither one of us is very happy any longer.

I'm sorry to bother you with this. No one wants to actually know such things about anyone else. We all have our own problems.

Maybe it's the same for everyone, but if so, this is a bad part of life. If it is that way for most people who've been married as long as Joanie and I, then I think it's unfair. This isn't how it should be. Joanie and I, after thirty-four years, should be bark on a tree at this point. Nothing should hurt us and we should be as tight as that. As usual, I have very little introspective power these days. Maybe if I tried harder I could see again like I used to and find a way to build a bridge that went backward and forward and get us out of here.

Without Joanie there isn't much left, and these days I don't know how to make that bridge. When I think about little Finn, and all his days burning with such a great light, I see my own going up in smoke, and the bridges collapsing both behind me and ahead. Past present future.

Chapter Four:
The Second Annual Almost-Memorial McMasters Run

One of the things that I have a difficult time with is trying to understand why the world is as confusing as it is. For those of you who read the news on a regular basis then I'm sure you get a daily dose of this, and probably you're facing degrading vertebrae from shaking your head so often, but I don't like venturing out much in that particular world so very often and so I'm usually pretty safe. Mostly.

As a single example of this strangeness let me tell you that it has been a ceaseless wonder to me to discover that there are actually quite a few people, wherever you go, who actually enjoy both sadness and fear. Yes, I understand entirely that fear and sadness are complete polar opposites to joy and happiness on the scale of human emotions. That's why I bring it up.

And yet, you know perfectly well that people will actually pay good money to make themselves sad. You've seen them: they're coming out of the theater and they're rubbing their eyes and they're just bawling and yet they're saying "That's the best movie I ever saw!" I realize that I'm not on the best and most stable of emotional grounds anymore, but that's just nuts if you ask me. Why would you want to intentionally see something that was very sad, and why in the world did you enjoy that? I just don't think I understand people very well any longer.

And don't even get me started about the folks who think fear is a good time and simply play a bit of linguistics and start calling it "thrilling". No, tying a giant rubber band around your legs and jumping off a cliff is not a way to spend your morning, unless, of course, you are one of those extremely strange people who live amongst us who confuse us all, most of the time.

Back in Oregon we had Smith Rock, and people came from all over the world just to try to kill themselves in plain view of an audience. Smith Rock is a series of peaks that rise inexplicably above an otherwise flat plain with what looks like, from up above, an itty-bitty creek meandering through it which in fact is the Crooked River and is not so itty-bitty at all, just to give you a Raven's-eye understanding of things.

From pinnacle-to-pinnacle are stretched cables, and when you climb the hundreds of feet up to one of them, why you can then walk out onto one of those one-inch cables and then have a very spectacular fall to an entirely unforgiving stop many hundreds of feet below. Like I said, folks come from all over the place to do this dance macabre, and then those who survive go home again. I just wanted to warn you that these people could possibly be your neighbors.

These same people live here in Montana I've come to discover. I thought I had run away from Crazy for good, but it seems as though it just follows you around. I'm not so sure how many people around here enjoy a good bit of sadness and weeping, because I've never asked them I guess, but when it comes to enjoying fear, then folks around here have it in Spades.

Around here there's all the fear a crazy person could want on a regular basis: getting caught up in the hay-baler and losing a few fingers or an arm, waiting to see every summer if a wildfire will sweep you and yours away in a towering flame, or maybe you just happen to be in the right place at the wrong time and find that giant rattlesnake, or Moose, or worse, a Grizzly, and then that's all she wrote about that. I won't even bother to mention rodeo, because that's Professional Fear, and so it comes in a category of inexplicability all by itself.

And yet, people live here. I do. It's great, despite being full of fear. The problem I have is when people go seeking it out. That's the problem.

In September, Chuck took me on down to The Paper on a Wednesday, which is when my column is due so it can come out that Saturday. When I walked into the office I found Jeff and Chip, each sitting at his desk, and both were obviously feeling pretty morose about something. Chip had his elbows on his desk and his chin cupped in both hands, and seemed to be looking blankly into space. Jeff was turned away from his desk, elbows on his knees, face similarly cupped in his hands, apparently staring at the wall.

"Hi guys, what's up? I'm just dropping off my column."

Neither said anything but Jeff sort of straightened himself up a bit and Chip sighed loudly.

"So what's the matter anyway?" I asked.

Chip leaned back in his chair and then said "We decided we won't do the McMasters run this year."

"We figured that after last year it was probably too dangerous to try again," Jeff said.

"And to top it off, it sounds like this year a whole bunch of people are interested in doing it," Chip added.

"And we can't even be part of it," Jeff lamented. "People from all over the place are contacting us about when the next race will be held and what the rules are and everything, and we can't even be part of it."

"Well, why not?" I asked. "It's your run after all. You guys built that slope. It's yours. Take charge of the race and host it. Make up some fun rules and prizes or trophies or something and send out news releases. You can be the big hosts of the race. You could even get a trophy named after yourselves to give to the winner."

Suddenly, both Chip and Jeff got up from their desks at the same time and looked at each other.

"We could!" Chip exclaimed.

"Yeah, it's our mountain after all," Jeff said. "We could call it the Second Annual Memorial McMasters Run and be in charge of the whole thing. That'd be fun!"

"Jeff, I think someone needs to die before it can be a Memorial-thing," Chip noted.

"Oh, right," Jeff said, a little deflated.

"Perhaps in honor of the fact that there are people who are glad no one died that day you could call it the Almost-Memorial Run?" I suggested.

Chip laughed. "That's sounds great."

January came once again as it always seems to do. There are years when I think we could just skip January and almost no one would really mind. The days were bitterly cold, and the nights would kill if you were unlucky enough to be out in one. The snow fell heavily at times. I found it oppressive. Jeff and Chip were delighted.

"It's perfect," Chip said, beaming, when I stopped by The Paper to ask how preparations were going. "It's absolutely perfect. We went out and checked out the slope today. It looks great."

"We've got everything set up too," Jeff said. "We've got food vendors and the EMT guys and two TV crews coming in from Missoula and Great Falls. Man, I wish Wide World of Sports was still going"

"Guess how many entries there are," Chip asked. "Eighty-three!" he answered.

I was shocked.

"Eighty-three!? How can there be eighty-three people willing to kill themselves and where are they coming from?"

Jeff picked up some papers and shuffled through them. "Well, there are some entries from here in town, but most of them are from all over the state. There are even some people coming from Minnesota and Washington and Nevada and even New Mexico."

I was duly impressed. "Wow. Who would have thought, huh? Did you get prizes or trophies or something?"

"Come on in the back," Chip said, and we all wandered back into the Warehouse of Broken Dreams where Chip and Jeff kept their contraptions from past and future competitions.

As we walked back Chip said, "We charged twenty bucks an entry. We thought that was sort of reasonable, and we wanted some nice trophies and stuff since people were coming from all over the place. So, we got first, second and third-place trophies, and then had money left for a thousand-dollar prize for the winner." Suddenly I was thinking if maybe I could go buy a sled somewhere.

"That's really great guys. I can just about guarantee that you'll have even more entries next year with that kind of prize money."

"Look at the trophies!" Jeff said as he switched on a light to reveal the snow-white trophies on a little table.

The biggest one, for the winner no doubt, was done as a classical loving cup, and on one side was an image of Chip in his saucer and on the other was Jeff in his tube. Inscribed at the top was the Second Annual Almost-Memorial McMasters Run.

All I could do was laugh. It was perfect, just like Chip said. Strangely, I was kind of excited about all of this. Maybe it was because I knew that my employers weren't going to be trying to kill themselves this year.

When the Saturday of the race arrived Joanie and I made sure we got there early. Real early. Chuck slip-slided up the mountain road at just about half-past dark and we parked and started hauling our gear out into the flats surrounding McMasters. We found a good spot about halfway down the run where you could see both the starting and finish lines, and we pitched our ice-fishing cabin. We pulled out lawn chairs and sat in the snow. Hollis and Kenna and Amy and Jill joined us, and we tailgated in style. Others were doing the same, and some brought grills and made food, while most of us bought food and drinks from the vendors. This year Joanie and I even indulged in a couple of "sled dogs" sold by the vendors, which I noticed had suddenly increased in price by three dollars from last year.

If last year people had been excited by the spectacle of something strange and interesting and yes, dangerous, to distract oneself in the middle of winter, this year the atmosphere was positively electric. If you hadn't gotten there early, you found yourself in the back trying to look over people's shoulders. I'm not real good with numbers, but I'm pretty sure the entire town was there, in addition to quite a few who had come from afar. There were three different news outfits there which had set up their gear up and then down the slope, and I figured these three probably covered all the channels you might get in Montana with a good antenna and a mountain-top home. Yep. It was really going to be something.

It is difficult to describe a genuine spectacle. There is so much happening all at once that I think it's probably only possible to tell it in bits and pieces, and I think I'll have to try again later to tell you all the rest of what I can remember from that day, but for a while let me tell you about how it started.

Chip and Jeff were of course the emcees for the competition, and even they were surprised by the turnout and enthusiasm. They had brought their banged up sleds up to the side of the slope so people could see the wreckage of last year's attempt, and before they knew it people were coming by and asking for autographs and can I get a photo of us next to your sled and this year's contestants were coming along and getting photos and autographs too and before you knew it, Dobbins had a couple of honest-to-goodness celebrities.

They were a bit chagrined about all the attention at first, but they quickly found that they were naturals at it. Of course, we townies wallowed in our association with them as often as possible when talking to new-comers: "Oh, Chip and Jeff, sure, best friends of mine. Why I remember when..." Like that.

The contestants themselves had descended on Dobbins during the past few days, and even though we do have an Inn in town, run by Esmerelda, it only has four rooms for rent and so folks offered to put them up in their own homes. Of the 83 people scheduled to risk their lives that day, only five were from Dobbins (maybe because we had all seen the year before what could happen to you) and so most of the contestants were from out of town. Fortunately, many had antici-pated the lack of lodging and had come with their RVs.

The day before the race, they had all brought their sleds out for public viewing, and you could now walk by each one and meet the man or woman who would being doing the run, and also check out their sleds. Chip and Jeff, and all the rest of us, quickly realized that next year there would also have to be a trophy for Most Outlandish Sled, because they had obviously in-spired a considerable amount of creativity with their own contraptions.

Almost everyone had some sort of custom-built sled, with only a very few exceptions, and there were some that, well, I'm uncertain if the builder actually intended to race or perhaps just go out of this world in a flame of artistic and eccentric glory. One woman had what appeared to be a surfboard to which she had mounted bull's horns, and explained that she had grown up on a ranch in the eastern expanses of the state, and that this was the only way she knew how to "steer". Another fellow had taken up Chip's flying saucer idea, but his also sported a rotating ring of flashing lights around the rim, and a plastic dome over the top. Still others had followed in Jeff's footsteps and had sleds that looked more like 1950's science fiction rocket ships. The crowd favorite, however, was an obvious choice: it was a giant wooden birdhouse resting on skis. I'm not making that up. The gentleman who sported this sled got inside for a photo shoot and kept sticking his head out a hole in the front and shouting "Cuckoo!" Kenna remarked that it seemed like the sled reflected its maker, and that this fellow had nailed it.

Jeff and Chip had established the rules for the race, and once again it would be done with pairs of contestants going down the slope at the same time. Pairs were chosen by lot, and when the guys realized how many runs would be taking place and how many people might reasonably actually make it all the way down, they established official timekeepers and even a photo finish. After all, they took this kind of thing very seriously in one way or another. If there were any ties, there would be a run-off to determine the winner.

But, the time eventually came when the race began, and I have to tell you, nobody who was watching who came and stood in the snow and the bitter cold for hours and who wished for a spectacle left that mountainside disappointed.

CHAPTER FIVE:
GENTLEMAN JACK

I forgot where I was there for a bit and I'm sorry about that. I think I was telling you about when Jack came to the house, and so let me get back to that for now. When Jack pulled into our place, both Joanie and I were a bit surprised. For one thing, as far as I know Jack doesn't frequent Dobbins very often, and for another he is almost always seen in the company of at least two of his army of hired hands. On top of this I was pretty certain that he wasn't here to talk about the column I wrote about him because he had called me after it had come out to express his pleasure with it and to thank me. And yet, here he was, walking up the drive with an expression on his face that suggested he was displeased about something, and that something appeared to reside at our place.

Jack made it to the porch and I greeted him with a handshake and then he turned to Joanie and doffed his hat and said "Joanie", which she admires very much in men but because I don't wear a hat I guess I can't imitate, and Joanie said "Can I get you some iced tea or a beer or something?" and Jack said "Do you have any Pinot Gris?" and Joanie said "I'm sure we do because that's my favorite," and Jack smiled his Gentleman

Smile and Joanie went inside and I motioned for Jack to take a seat there on the porch.

On any given day these days I get confused about one thing or another, as if something in my head just isn't firing on all cylinders or something, and I suppose I've gotten used to that enough that I don't really notice it all that much any longer. But this had me stumped and sitting on my own front porch I was a bit concerned I guess because this was Jack Jackson and he was here for A Reason.

Master-of-Conversation that I am, I said "So what's new Jack? Those new cows you bought are doing okay are they?"

"Doing very well," Jack said, looking at me keenly, and it was the kind of look that a hawk gives a sparrow. To my relief Joanie reappeared with a glass of wine for Jack and so now, I presumed, we could talk.

"Thanks for coming by," Joanie said, and right about there my heart soared with admiration for her because I couldn't think of a blasted thing to say. "We don't get so many visitors it seems," Joanie continued.

And Gentleman Jack, ever the man of courtesy said, "I'm surprised, given that you live here," looking at Joanie.

Unfortunately, that bit of flirting just went right over my head right then and I only realized it later, or I'd have asked Jack to, well, I'm not sure, but something.

Well, I could be a bit jealous when it comes to Joanie, but I had to ask: "What can we do for you Jack?" and that's when he set his glass of wine down and said "I need to tell you a story". And so he did.

Jack and his wife, who's Navajo, met and fell in love

down at Bluff, in Utah when Jack was younger and wandering and just passing through. He met Haseya when she was a waitress at the Navajo Twins restaurant, just below the towering rocks there. Jack had been sitting at an outside table, watching the hummingbirds feeding on the trumpet flowers in the first light, sipping a cup of coffee when Haseya came by to take his order.

The way Jack says it, it was love at first sight, and Jack told her that he had big plans and wanted to buy some land where he could be happy and raise cattle and find peace and have a family, and that he had some money saved up and he was travelling to see where he wanted to be. Haseya said that sounded good to her, and they got in Jack's truck and headed over to a chapel nearby and got married, and then Haseya said they'd better do things the Right Way, and so they went back to Bluff and got married again with all her family in attendance. That took about a week or so. Then they got on the road.

The way Jack tells it, they zigged and zagged and then found their way into Montana at some point, and Haseya said this felt very good to her and Jack thought so too, and so they sort of moseyed around until they found where they wanted to be and they said this was it and so that was that.

As it happened, Jack's father was the owner of an enormous shoe factory in Illinois, and when he died he bequeathed everything to Jack. Jack said that he had nothing against continuing to run an operation like that, and had done so through his twenties along with his father, but he always felt that he wanted to do something a bit more challenging than an industry in a factory, and had been sort of "outside-minded", as he said, from an early age. Not to put too fine a point on it, but when Jack met Haseya he didn't actually mention the fact that he'd just told the board of directors back in Illinois that he was cashing out his end of the family fortune and that they could carry on just fine without him, and that he was a wealthy man.

The way he tells it is that he came into Dobbins and discovered that two different ranchers were getting on in years and had no offspring to speak of and so he bought it all, quite a few thousand acres, and he kept this on the down-low from Haseya because he said he didn't want her to think he was some sort of dude rancher or something like that.

So, he moved them into a tiny little house out somewhere on all that land, because he's afraid to tell her what's going on, even though he could have built them a palace. Well, he got the land but along with that came all the cattle that were still on it, and he had thousands of acres to cover by himself. At first he just reveled in the work of doing everything by himself, and he said he learned everything at that point and he actually got to like his cows, onery and willful things that that are.

Then, at some point, coming home at midnight from a long day and exhausted, Haseya confronted him and asked where he'd been all day and Jack figured he'd better finally tell her the truth of all this and so he did and he expected Haseya to give him an earful, but she didn't, and instead she sat down at their little table in their little kitchen and made him sit down too.

"You have told me some stories I see, yes?

And Jack hung his head and said "Yes, but I just didn't want you to..."

And Haseya interrupted him and said, "I'd like to tell you a story too. Just a short one." And so she did. Jack listened.

Haseya told Jack about a time among the Navajo when all the water went away and the crops died and the people were starving and there was nothing to be done. The various versions of the Wise Men were consulted and nothing could be done. The people suffered. She said that one day, a mother had to bury her child because he hadn't had enough to eat, and when she was burying him, her tears burrowed into the dry ground and from them, a spring bubbled up and ran everywhere. She said that her husband was amazed and said that they should quickly build up a dike so that they could keep this good luck to themselves, but the wife said that tears belong to us all and let the water flow so that all could drink and live again.

The way Jack tells it, and he's just finished his pinot gris and Joanie pours him another half glass, is that he sat at the table for a bit just looking at his wife and then he stood up and said "I understand", and that was kind of it because Jack just starting hiring everyone and anyone and building them little places here and there all over his land and they worked for him and if you ever saw Jack on his own place, like I have, surrounded by his men and women, you'd know in an instant that these are not "employees", but rather his people, his friends, his neighbors, and they would do anything for him and Haseya. There is a bond there that cannot be explained in a simple word like "gratitude". No, Jack and Haseya have an enormous family on their part of our county.

And Joanie asked when he paused what I wanted to ask because all I could do was listen, "But what are you doing here Jack? What do you want?"

And Jack said, looking at his glass, and with his quiet voice, "I just want understanding is all and I think some things have been misunderstood and I wanted you to know. That's all."

And so he went on a bit more. He said that one day he was out baling hay somewhere in the expanses of his realm and Haseya had come with him and she was very unhappy with all the machines needing to do the work, because they caused quite a ruckus of course, but that she understood as well that the work had to be done, and that many were depending on the hay.

They had stacked the bales in that particular field, and Jack said that it was real nice to see their work done, and he and Haseya and quite a few of Jack's men came and had a bit of a picnic out there, and watched the rest of the day go by.

So anyway, the sun was getting low then and everyone was so very pleased with the day's work and Haseya said, while watching the sun go to sleep over a gigantic stack of bales, "They seem so very unnatural, don't they Jack? As if they didn't belong among our very large family."

Jack stood up, looked around, and said "You're right. I think I want something more, I don't know, more natural somehow. What do you think my love?"

"Whatever you think is best my love," Haseya said.

Jack paused there and looked at me and Joanie and said, "So, you see, it had to be round bales. Nothing else would do."

"Sure, I get it," Joanie said. "I think you're wife was right too. I like round hay bales, now that I think about it."

Jacked positively beamed at her.

"Me too, Jack," I said. "I even mentioned them in the column just like you asked."

And at that, Jack's smile went away and he said, looking hard at me, "Then why did you write a column the very next week in which you wrote that Einar's were so much better than mine?"

"What?! I didn't, I just wrote about his hay bale sculpture is all! I didn't say they were better. I didn't compare yours to his."

Jack stood then and sort of squinted at me.

"You have to understand. There can only be one kind of bale in this county, and it's going to be round. It's the only good thing to do, and that's it." He doffed his hat to Joanie and said "Joanie," with a slight bow, "thanks for the wine. It was very good. It was a pleasure." And then he walked back to his truck and drove away.

"What'd you do this time?" Joanie asked.

38

CHAPTER SIX:
THE SMARTEST KID YOU'LL EVER KNOW

I'm pretty sure everyone has their opinions about kids. I think the phrase I heard most often while a kid myself was "Kids these days," always said with a tone that blended undisguised disappointment with a touch of genuine surprise, and which also included a sort of sad shaking of the head. People have been saying this same thing for time out of mind, way before The Beatles and Elvis, and even Socrates bemoaned the foibles of the youth of Athens during the fifth century BC.

As I got older I continued to hear this phrase, and sometimes nodded in commiseration with the speaker (of course glad that it was no longer directed at myself), but I grew to understand that this opinion of kids, at least for the most part, has largely been a matter of adults forgetting what it was like to be a kid. Well, for the most part.

Around Dobbins I sometimes find myself wondering what childhood might actually be like. For one thing, you often don't see many kids around because they mostly live on ranches and farms and probably spend at least a fair bit of their day with the unending chores that come with such a life. I imagine that's a good thing for the most part. I'm guessing anyway. Of course I know Theo and Simon from down at Gil's, and of course when they're working they're sort of on-stage if you know what I mean, transporting tourists into raptures of 50's nostalgia. Mind you, that's only during the summers and the rest of the time they get to be kids.

To tell the truth, I really don't know what being a kid around here is like, but I do know Morningstar Jackson, and she's the smartest kid you'll ever know.

The story goes that Morningstar, who's the daughter of Jack and Haseya, showed herself to be a prodigy somewhere around the third grade. She'd had one of those What Did You Do on Your Summer Vacation tasks presented to her in the fall, and she responded with a thesis something along the lines of Americans getting soft and too entitled and not working hard enough to accomplish their dreams, and if you really wanted to succeed in life then you'd better work your butt off instead of going on a summer vacation. I am paraphrasing, of course.

Anyway, this sort of thing coming from the daughter of one of the most powerful and, admittedly, hardest working people in the county, there was considerable doubt as to the authorship of said paper, and the fact that it had textual citations and a references page in proper APA style was sort of the clincher. However, as it also happened, the second grade teacher was in the teacher's lounge when this was brought to light and defended Morningstar as her brightest pupil. This announcement was accompanied by certain looks and then a challenge to find out just how smart she really was (or wasn't, as was the intention), because there was no way on God's green earth that anyone was going to call up Jack Jackson and tell him his daughter had been caught cheating at school.

So, Morningstar's third-grade teacher began giving her quizzes and tests from the fourth-grader's classes, and she aced them. This caused some consternation in the teacher's lounge, but many were not convinced. They did this again and again apparently, handing her exams about things that none of the kids had been learning anything about, and she aced those too.

Finally, one of the main naysayers announced that he thought it was all a hoax and anybody could get lucky on a quiz or an exam, and that the real test should be an in-class essay. So, that's what they did, and every third grader got an assignment to write on there in the classroom, and they gave Morningstar a "special" one. She was to write about how people in America had become more polarized during the past few decades, and one wag announced that he couldn't wait to see if she wrote about Montana winters.

When she was done, the teacher picked it up and took it to the lounge for inspection after classes were over for the day. She read aloud to the stunned audience as Morningstar's treatise on the causes and effects of social and political divisions were laid out one by one. At the end, Morningstar closed her essay with a brief question, asking why she was being given quizzes and tests and assignments that no one else was being given, but also added that she didn't mind because she thought they were much more interesting than what she had been doing. Silence in the room.

Then, her greatest naysayer stood up, apologized to everyone, and said "Wow. We have a real-live genius on our hands! I think it's fantastic!"

Everyone agreed, and everyone wanted to help in any way they could. Presently, at the ripe old age of thirteen, she has completed most of the general education courses for college, and trust me, colleges are drooling over her. Kenna once told me that Morningstar's father had said she'd already received offers from Stanford and Harvard, among others, and he had wondered aloud if it was because she was both African-American and also Native-American and if the schools thought they would score some big diversity and multicultural points with her in attendance. I don't know about that, but I do know that Morningstar is the real deal.

The first time I met Morningstar happened to be a time when Chuck was slightly under the weather for some reason nothing serious I imagine, but just not quite at his usual tip-top self, and I had pulled up next to the curb in town and had popped the hood to see if there was anything I could see. The problem there is that, well, I'm not quite sure how to say it politely so I won't, I just don't know pretty much anything about what's going on under the hood of a vehicle, or any other part of its anatomy for that matter.

So, when this little girl with a ponytail and her jeans rolled up above her ankles and sporting white Chuck Taylors pulled to a stop—on her bicycle and asked if I needed any help, I wasn't exactly sure what to say. If it had been an adult I might have tried to explain the funny noise I'd been hearing and waited to be enlightened by their much vaster knowledge of engines than my own. But this was a little kid with a very serious face who was waiting for an answer and that sort of threw me off for a bit.

Eventually I said "Oh, thank you for stopping, but I was just checking something and it should be fine."

She did not in fact head on her way. Instead, she looked at me as if I was somehow lying to her, with her head cocked just a bit, eye-balling me, kind of maybe the way Hollis does sometimes.

"You're Al and this is Chuck, right?" she asked.

I was only a little surprised by that because Chuck was famous, and maybe she knew my name simply in association with his.

"Yes, this is Chuck," I said, patting him a couple of times.

"I thought so," she said. "So Chuck's a '72 right? Early and rare version of their extended cab line? Only 500 if I'm not mistaken. 327 engine, right?"

I didn't say anything, but kind of just stupidly looked at her again. She just cocked her head again and looked at me, as if that might be the only angle from which I made sense.

"So what's up with him?"

I wasn't very sure what I was facing here, so I simply said what I'd been hearing, describing it as best I could.

"Two barrel carb, right?" she asked.

I didn't know the answer to that and she seemed to know that as if "stupid" was printed in large letters on my forehead.

"That's okay," she said. "You have a screwdriver? Flat-head?"

I went around and looked in my little toolbox that I

keep in the back, and sure enough I had one, which I produced and showed her.

"Now what?" I asked.

"Easier if I do it myself than explain, but watch."

She got off her bike and put down the kickstand and I handed her the screwdriver and she scrambled up the bumper and into the engine compartment which only a blasted thirteen-year-old could do and I was jealous, and she said "See that little screw there on the distributor?" and she put the screwdriver in place and turned it counter-clockwise, "it's just the timing is a bit off. Try it now."

So, she got down and I turned the key, and sure enough, I didn't hear the noise I'd been hearing before and good ol' Chuck just purred.

I got out and came around and I thanked her and she smiled and put out a hand, "Name's Morningstar," she said. "Glad to help."

We shook hands and then she got on her bike and headed down the sidewalk with a backward wave, and I got back to Chuck and sat there for a minute wondering what in the world had happened to the world.

CHAPTER SEVEN:
THE GREAT DIVIDE

Our little house, which sits up on the eastern ridge, which is only one of four, and looks down on Dobbins down below just maybe a scant two miles away, and Dobbins looks as if it were scooped out of a giant's ice cream bowl, is somewhat of a geographical wonder. I say this because on three sides, we're surrounded by the Continental Divide which essentially separates East from West. It just zigs and zags around our place. Joanie and I, and most of the folks who reside here, have our minds made up about which side of the divide we're on. Besides, we're so far from anything that anyone might consider "East" that you'd have to flip a whole bunch of pages in your atlas to see. Our house sits exactly 5280 feet above sea level, exactly a mile. I measured it with an altimeter once out of curiosity. I also once mentioned this to Delmer, our neighbor and the town banker, and he said his place was five feet higher than that, and he looked at me and smiled. Bankers.

Living in this particular location is special, as you might imagine. You're up high. You see everything, or at least you should I suppose. We watch the elk herds come and go, and try to keep the antelope away from our two pathetic tomato plants we do each year, hoping against hope that we might get a couple, maybe just a couple of nice ones for the BLT's of our dreams, with such a short season. The moose stomp through the back yard and if you try to shoo them away they simply look at you, and if the bull is there then that look says "You and whose army?" We live up here because so does life. It's everywhere in all directions. You can't help but see it in summer, and miss it in winter. It's all around you and you see and are aware of it. It is so wonderful seeing all this, all the time. I love it here.

Not long ago another of those summer thunderstorms came through, and I was looking out the window from the house at it, and at this elevation I wasn't so very surprised to see Zeus and Thor walking down our driveway which is pretty much in someone else's upper airs, old buddies, just catching up again. Yep. This is it. You're all in on it or nothing.

That winter I could see it in Joanie, in every little thing she said and did or didn't do or say, and what I saw reflected back on me was that I wasn't much there anymore, not to her way of seeing. I'm sure other people saw me, or at least I think so, but Joanie couldn't see me any longer. That hurt and I didn't yet understand why.

Joanie and I were playing a game of Scrabble and she was getting all the good words.

At some point she said "What's going on with you? You keep saying you can't make a word. Let me see your letters."

And then she did and she plunked them down on the board and said "What about this?" And then she picked them up and put some of them somewhere else and said "What about this?"

And then she did it again and looked at me to see if I could see what she'd done and I said "It's upside down. What does that spell?"

And then she swept the tiles off the board and went in the other room and I put the game away.

Joanie spends much of her time now in the front room with the dogs and the television. She watches TV for maybe eight or nine hours a day, or maybe just has it on. I don't know. When she's not she's searching for things on her computer. She's looking for things that she wants to see and hear.

I spend most of my time in my little room. I'm not sure what I want to see and hear. I can almost remember. There's something there that I can't feel or see any longer. Past present future.

CHAPTER EIGHT:
GEORGE TELLS ME SOMETHING UNUSUAL

Probably the person I talk the most to these days other than Joanie and Chuck is George, and almost always down at Del's. We unofficially meet for coffee several times each week and we sit on the stools at the counter pretending we have things to do and are just taking a break from doing them. George has a tack shop in town, but most people get their stuff at the Coastal, so he tends on average to have as much time on his hands as I do. He just has a sign on the door of his shop that everyone knows which says, in short, if you want something, give me a call and I'll be there in ten minutes.

The first time I met George I knew we were going to hit it off because he has this absolutely artistic sense of sarcastic and cynical humor. I was sitting at the counter at Del's when he came in and parked himself on the stool next to me.

He looked at me and said, "Seen you around. You're Al, right? With Chuck?"

Chuck is of course famous for having been in The Paper, while I merely write for it, so he's kind of my foot in the door with most people in the county. Anyway, George introduces himself as George Onacona and tells me has a tack shop called "White Owl" because that's what Onacona means in Cherokee and that he thought White Owl sounded a whole lot cooler for tourists than Onacona, and I had to agree.

He finished this by saying "Whites are just crazy about Indian stuff."

And then he looked at his coffee and said "I guess they're just stupid or something because you can get pretty much the same stuff at the Coastal as at my place, I just charge more, and yet they keep calling me all the time in summer." And he looked at me and said "No offense, you know."

I said, "No, I've run into that from time to time myself."

So I asked him if he's Cherokee, and by golly he sure looks like it, and he said yes and I asked him where he grew up and he looked at me like I was really stupid but went ahead and said Oklahoma anyway, and so I asked him what I always ask everyone and that's why are you in Dobbins of all the places one might be in the world.

"Oh, I have family out here so I moved."

"Really? I haven't seen any other Cherokee folks out here. Where do they live?"

"Over in Missoula or thereabouts."

"What? That's over 200 miles from here. I thought you moved here because of family."

"Yeah, but I can't stand them."

He looked kind of sideways at me, and I started to grin, and then he did too, and then we're both laughing so hard we couldn't drink our coffee.

One morning when I showed up at Del's and saw George already there, I came up and sat down and he said, "Al, I've been thinking about this for a long time now and I need to tell someone and you're going to be it."

He had a serious expression on his face that I didn't think I had seen before and I didn't, for once, think he was going to tell me some dry joke, as was our usual fare.

"Okay. What?"

"I'm tired of being Cherokee," he said, and he looked away. He looked down at his coffee for a bit and turned to me and said "I think I'm tired of being Native American I guess."

Now, I have to pause a bit here and tell you that my brain these days just doesn't fire in the same way that it used to just a few years ago, and so things take me a while to process. I could tell you about what I think happened there to my head, but that's a whole different story and I don't feel like telling it here. I think I'll just tell you instead that when George said that, there was simply no sense in it and yet I wanted to make sense of it, so in my very highly trained, college professor analytical mind, I said "What?" with some level of disbelief at what I'd heard.

"I'm serious," he said. "I'm tired of being looked at as something different from anyone else, and I'm tired of trying to parley being an Indian into something, just sort of taking advantage of it, and I'm just tired of it. Did you know I got a full ride at the University of Oklahoma just because I'm native?"

I shook my head, but said "So what? That's great isn't

it? I'd have liked that. I'm still paying on my student loans by the way."

George slapped his hand on the counter and said "That's what I'm talking about! That's what I came up here for. I just want to be anybody and nobody and make my own way and be my own man and you can't if you're different in some obvious way! And around here I'm about as obvious as it gets. I don't care about 'fitting in' or something like that, I just want to not be something that, you know, is like taking advantage of others just because of who I am."

I didn't know what in the world to make of this, and I might have taken an hour and a half to remind George of exactly who had been taking advantage of whom for the past 400 years, but for some reason I didn't because I didn't know what to think. This wasn't something I'd have expected anyone to say, let alone George.

This was maybe the craziest conversation I'd had in a few years, not counting talks with Chip and Jeff, except I could tell he was truly serious, and I don't know if that's ever happened to you or maybe it's just me, and yes, it's just me, but when confronted with the serious I just don't seem to handle it all too well anymore, and besides, this was George, so I said: "There's a joke about that."

"About what?"

"About wanting to switch nationalities," I said.

"Let's hear it."

"Umm, well, who is okay to make fun of anymore? Kind of tricky there these days if I understand correctly."

George thought about that for a minute and then

said "Swedes. They seem pretty safe don't you think? I mean, you don't hear anything from the Swedish Anti-Defamation League do you?"

"Okay, Swedes, that seems okay. So, anyway, there's this Swede who for whatever reason doesn't want to be Swedish any longer. He's tired of all the Swedish Chef jokes from The Muppets or something. All this 'Ja and Ja and stoof the turkey' and all that. So, he decides he wants to be Italian instead, because he thinks being Italian would be really nice. So, he goes on into town to start his first day of being Italian and he goes to the store and says, because he's been studying up, 'I'd like some linguini, cavatelli, and a good bottle of Barbera.' Well, the store owner looks at him and says 'You're Swedish aren't you?' And then the poor fellow, abashed, says 'How did you know?' And then the shop-keeper says 'Well, for one thing, this is a hardware store.'"

George turned and looked at me, and he said "I don't gct it."

And about five seconds go by and then we are laughing so hard that Del comes out from the back and gives us a look sort of like I Will Not Tolerate Drunks nor Ne'er-Do-Wells in my place, and so we tried to just snigger into our hands for a little bit.

Anyway, after we settled ourselves a bit, at least so Del wasn't glaring at us anymore, I said, "Okay, I've got it."

Whatever the heck it is he's thinking, which I can't understand at all, I figure what the heck, I'll play along I guess. So, I look him over and George has what to me are pretty obviously "classical" looks. He's in his 30's I suppose, and he has what used to be called "jet-black" hair, except no one knows anymore what "jet" is and so I'll say instead his hair is, his hair is, well, it's like the blackest of black and if it was growing out of my own head I'd have it several feet long and swept around my neck like a scarf. He doesn't. He should. And then his nose! His cheekbones! He looks like a young Julius Caesar. He's tall and lean and fit.

And what I say is "Greek."

"What? Greek?"

"I know what I'm talking about here George. Yeah, Greek. The nose, the hair, the build. Yep. I saw you once in *The Iliad.* Uh huh, you're the long-lost son of an ancient mariner who made it to our shores and didn't know the world was round, though of course the Greeks were the first to point that out to humanity."

"But Greek?"

"You'll have to dress a little differently," I said, "even for Montana. Go home and look yourself up online, and then maybe you'll meet a Greek heiress or something and start dating."

George looked thoughtful, which was probably not what I'd expected. Anyway, because I really can't take too much craziness at a time these days, I think I'll just leave it at that for now.

Chapter Nine:
There Are Only So Many Marshmallows In A Box Of Lucky Charms

Did you know that there are over seven-hundred known versions of the story most of us think of as "Cinderella"? It's true. Folklorists and ethnologists have been recording all these various stories for many decades now. What's really interesting is that this particular story has been told all over the world since at least the Middle Ages, and by people who never had any historical contact with one another.

That's right. It seems like everyone was telling the same story in one version or another, all at the same time. Native Americans were telling their versions of the same story, even while Jakob and Wilhelm Grimm were prowling the German countryside recording stories told to them by the local peasantry. People living in the South Seas were telling it at the same time people in China and Ireland were telling it. Humanity seems to have spontaneously made it up together somehow.

Various individuals have posited their theories about how this could possibly have happened, and some, like

Carl Jung, thought that maybe humanity had some sort of collective memory, back from the very beginning, and that somehow we all tapped into the same memory, at about roughly the same time. Maybe so. We all know the story, wherever we are. As soon as you start to tell the version you know to someone else, they just start nodding their head. Yes, of course. I know that story.

Now mind you, things are always a little different from one version of the story to another. Sometimes it's not golden or glass slippers the prince has to identify his bride-to-be. It could be a scarf, or a bracelet, or something else entirely, and things like that.

Anyway, what's really interesting here is that while you and I are used to fairy tales ending with two young people getting married at the end, and the final line being "and they lived happily ever after," just about half of the time these stories don't end that way at all. They just don't. They don't end happily ever after and there's some other kind of thing the storyteller wants us to understand.

Sometimes I'm amazed at the insight of humanity.

One morning I stopped in at Kenna's Curl Up and Dye to get my hair cut, and most of the regulars who made up Kenna's audience were there. In particular, I saw that Dreama was there with her daughter Athena, sitting directly in front of where Kenna was holding forth, telling some story or another to her rapt audience, and presumably cutting an elderly lady's hair.

Just as a matter of describing part of the scene, one could hardly imagine that Athena and Dreama were related, let alone mother and daughter. Dreama was wearing her typical Army sweatshirt with the sleeves cut off, the better to flex her huge biceps, and was sporting Montana-standard jeans and boots. Her hair was done as a sort of gray crew-cut, razor-sharp on all sides as far as I could tell. In contrast, thirteen-year-old Athena was absolutely impeccably dressed in a polka-dot dress with shiny black vinyl belt and black-strapped glossy shoes, and she had long dark hair, done in a large bow in the back and was made up in such a way as to resemble a child star from a 50's movie of some sort, probably also involving a teenage Mickey Rooney. She would be perfect hanging out at Gil's.

In any case, I had just walked in on something that Kenna was saying, and she had a very serious look on her face. She saw me but didn't make eye contact for some reason, maybe because she was so worked up at the moment, but it seemed as though she and Dreama were going back and forth about something.

Dreama says "Well, I don't quite get it. What'd he do?"

Kenna stops what she's doing and points her scissors at Dreama and says "That ain't nobody's business but my own, but I can say that he's the most stone-hearted, stone-headed jughead I ever met, and the thing is, he acts like he doesn't even know it! He acts like he can't understand or somethin'! He can't listen to anything. It's like he's just goin' around singin' 'Lalalalalalala I caaaaan't heaaaaar you' or somethin'!"

There is a small voice from somewhere in the audience, and I turn to see that it is Maude, and she says with her eyes not looking at Kenna, "Well, that's going to happen my dear. I mean, well," and Maude, who's I don't know, she's older than me anyway, says "that's the way things go. You know, up and down, all the time. It's just the way things go"

Kenna looks at her, and shifts to put all her weight on one leg and points her scissors in Maude's direction as if maybe they were a magic wand or something, and says "Well, it ain't happenin' to me, and that's that."

And then Kenna turned and made a snip at the elderly lady's hair, and a largish lock fell to the floor. Kenna looked down at it and frowned, but began snipping again anyway, a little more conservatively.

Dreama said, "Well, so then what?"

Kenna, who I know is now just pretending to size up both sides of the elderly lady's hair, and finding that if she leans a certain way they line up just fine, just stands up straight with her back to her audience, pretending she's involved with hair-cutting, and says "So I threw the big lug out the door and I haven't seen him since."

"Well, when was that?" Dreama asked.

"Three weeks ago," Kenna said quietly, at least for her.

Crazily, Athena starts crying and it's ruining her makeup, and Dreama just looks from Athena to Kenna and scowls a bit, and Kenna now has her back to everyone and is looking intently at her hair cutting, and I am only now figuring out what Kenna has been talking about.

I clear my throat and say, "Kenna, I just remembered something I have to do, would you mind too much if I came back tomorrow?"

And I see her look up and we see each other in the mirror and there is both grief and gratitude in her expression, and she makes a faint smile that took some effort and says "Thanks, Al. That'd be real good."

I went home and told Joanie and she said that that was too bad, "But he's a big boy and I'm sure he'll figure it out. Or maybe he won't," and then she just walked out of the room.

That wasn't the reaction I was expecting, at all.

Later on, Chuck and I drove over to Wiley's Wreck-A-Mended and there was Hollis' truck, parked up by the office. I went up to the door and went on inside, but no Wiley and no Hollis either. There was a desk and an old phone on it, and some shop manuals so smeared with oil and grease that they were likely illegible, but of course to me they would have been so even brand new.

I walked through the dilapidated Quonset hut and made my way out the back door where I found Wiley wiping his hands with a shop cloth and looking sadly at an equally sad looking vehicle of some sort.

"Hi Wiley, how's it going? I just stopped in to see Hollis is all. I saw his truck out front."

Wiley, if it was possible, looked even sadder than his normal world-woe at this and only said "I don't know where he is. I haven't seen him in almost three weeks. One morning I got here and saw his truck and so I thought he'd just come in early that day, but he wasn't here. I don't know where he is. It's like he just walked off somewhere. I called Kenna and she didn't help much, and she didn't seem very worried either. That was maybe over two weeks ago." Wiley shook his head.

"That's bad," was all I could say, but I filled him in on the fact that he and Kenna were obviously not getting along and that she had thrown him out of the house. After that I drove home, wondering where he could have gone. If anyone ever wanted to get lost, Montana was for sure the place to do it.

CHAPTER TEN:
A GHOST IN THE MOUNTAINS

If you ever met me you'd find that I am a very ordinary person. I have a job, I am married and love my wife, we have dogs and a house and I drive a pickup truck. I go fishing whenever I can. That's about it. Mind you, that's all the stuff you can largely see on the outside I guess, and so, who knows? Maybe I'm more complicated on the inside? Or maybe not. It's hard to say anymore.

One thing I can say about myself that maybe you can't see by looking is that ever since the shooting at my school and its aftermath and my decision to run away from it all and move to Dobbins of all places, I have been kind of confused about things. Actually, now that I think about it, I tend on average to be confused about a lot of things. I guess I don't really think all that much about being confused if I can help it. That's just the way it's going right now.

Anyway, what I'm really trying to say is that when I learned that Kenna had kicked Hollis out of the little house they'd bought in town after they had gotten married in the spring and that apparently Hollis was as good as missing for almost a month and no one had seen him, then yes, that confused me. I didn't know what to think or even feel about that. There really wasn't much I could do about it on any end of things, and so what was left was just helplessness.

Because there isn't much more I can say about that right now I'm going to tell you instead that ever since that shooting I have found myself wanting to be out fishing as often as I can. I've always loved fishing, especially fly fishing, but as life has changed for me fishing has changed for me as well.

It's difficult for someone like me to say, who has no craft with words, but I think it's all about The River. The moving water is restless, never stopping, wild and volatile, changing shape as it flows across the land and is a thing untamed and cannot be shaped to anyone's will. It comes and it goes, despite what you might want, and where it goes is its own way in everything.

It billows up here and there, foaming and surging and breaking over and around boulders, waters perhaps a gentle touch on the tops of stone, wearing them down bit by bit, crashing through canyons and throwing itself off cliffs in complete abandon and disregard for anything but itself and there's no stopping its force. It cannot be denied.

Elsewhere it can eddy out into sleepy pools, deep or shallow, and the air above it is electrified with life. It is Life. It is a life so big and powerful that it really can't be imagined by one such as me.

I just like to stand in it, curling around me as though we shared something, like one of our dogs fondly rubbing itself against my legs. It means something to me, this Life, and I cleave to it as to almost nothing else, and I hope it might cleave to me as well. It is soothing, beautiful beyond words, dangerous, unpredictable, in a hurry, peaceful. It is life. It breaks and makes.

There came a morning when I was standing before the river in the near-dark, waiting for just a little more of the light so that I could walk into an unfamiliar stretch of The River, whichever one it was, and I was waiting. I wasn't really thinking about anything at all, which is how it goes for me these days, I was just waiting for the light. And then, oddly, I did see a light, up above the ridge on the other side of the river, a light that was not sunlight. It flickered, grew, and died down as I watched it, a fire on the ridge here in the middle of nowhere. I couldn't think about it very long however, because of the river you see, and so I waded in when I could and then everything else was swept away to wherever it must go.

I cast for some while, all my attention on the tiny fly at the end of my line, and I caught several nice fish, and I let each one go, as gently as I could, back to the current of their place in things. At times I just stopped to stand in the water, not thinking so much about anything, but just standing there. Other times I watched dragonflies and damselflies navigate the currents, less than an inch above the rolling waters, marveling that they were neither caught by the waters nor the fish. They obviously knew what they were doing, while for me, I just stood and watched. At some point I decided I wanted to tie on another fly, and so made my way back to the bank and sat on a suitable rock to do so. As the sun crested the ridge in front of me I was reminded of the earlier light I had seen, and looked up again.

There, on the rock-strewn ridge, quite a long ways off from me, a tall man stood. He was dressed in black as near as I could tell from where I sat. I knew him, I was sure of that, but I had no idea what to do. I could see he was looking at me, and I raised my arm. He stood there for a while, looking down on me from far away, and though he wore no hat his arm arced up briefly as if to touch the rim of one, and then the sun crested the ridge and obliterated my view and when I could see again he was gone.

CHAPTER ELEVEN:
VICTORY

I tend to get overwhelmed easily these days. It doesn't really seem to matter what it is, but if there's too much of anything going on at once I can't seem to take it all in and then I just sort of shut down for awhile. Not long ago I found myself standing next to a river as I was preparing to fish, and I realized I had been standing there for some little time, not doing anything but just looking out onto nothing in particular, and then I remembered that I'd been trying to decide which fly to tie on. I looked down and there was my open fly box in my hand, and there were just too many to think about and so I looked away. That's how it's going these days. Maybe that's why I stopped telling you about the McMasters run. It was really too much to take in, but I wouldn't have missed it for anything.

It was very cold but none of us cared. As the minutes rolled by, growing ever closer to noon, the anticipation was as crisp as the air and those of us who'd been sitting and chatting with others or meandering back and forth to the food vendors now stood up and found our places along the run. Right at Noon, Delmer came on over the loudspeaker set up at the starting line and welcomed both contestants and spectators to the

competition. He laid out the rules and assured everyone of the timekeepers and then that was pretty much
it. A big cheer went up from the crowd and the EMT
guys were on their toes, and then the runs began.

With over forty pairs of people scheduled to head
down the slope, I can only give you some highlights.
The way it started was right from the get-go the first
two pairs had like, I don't know, but "real" sleds and
they were here to make it and win. Well, what happened at first was kind of what everyone expected I
think, because one guy went straight down and
whang! went right into the first boulder and the EMT
guys were scrambling up the slope to check him out,
but the second guy he seemed to know what he was
doing and he slowed down some and went around
the first boulder and then he picked up speed and
when he got to the second big old rock then he
slowed down and got around it too and then he was
pell mell for the finish line and we had our very first
person to actually cross it and a big cheer went up
from the crowd!

The next pair lined up at the top and down they went,
and then the next after them. Many of the contestants
who had somewhat more outlandish contraptions
dragged their feet down the slope, or even got off at
times to manage their way around the boulders, and
seemed more intent on just being able to walk away in
one piece and say that they had made the run. Others,
however, were clearly more competitive.

A pair of this last sort lined up in sleds nearly identi-
cal to one another, things that looked almost like
kayaks with skis out front and rudders in the rear.

With my binoculars I could sort of see them looking at one another, and the looks weren't very friendly. They both had a big push from the guys at the top and down they went. It wasn't more than seconds, however, when you could tell there was some bad blood going on here, because both of them seemed more intent on ramming each other if they could than worry overmuch about the slope. We were all given a speeded up version of the chariot race from *Ben Hur.*

When they got close enough to one another, and they both had the same kind of sled and so were going about the same speed, they'd try to bang into one another and set the other one off course. Somehow they both managed to navigate the first boulder, but when they reached about midway, where we were standing, then they banged each other really hard and the one on the left went cart-wheeling into the trees, but the other came flying off the slope directly at us.

All of us ducked and scattered as best we could, and here came this guy, still strapped in his sled as if he were still trying to steer it, and landed in the middle of us. His sled came down nose-first and his restraints broke and he came flying out of his sled and collided with Jill, who said "Oof!" and the guy landed right on top of her!

Before any of us could react, the guy scrambled to his feet and picked Jill up in his arms and yelled "Medic!" but Jill was fine and asked him to set her down and he did so with great relief and told her again and again how sorry he was. He said his name was Anders, which means "manly" in Swedish if you didn't know, and that "he would do anything to make amends."

Jill looked up at him and smiled, because this guy was maybe six-four and no bean-pole, and said, thoughtfully, "Okay."

"You're okay then?" he asked.

"Yes, but what about the other guy?" Jill said.

"It's my stupid brother," Anders shrugged. "I'm sure he'll be fine."

Anyway, after that little bit of excitement the races resumed. Again and again the contestants went down the slope, and sometimes we cheered or laughed or said "Oh!" or just held ourselves still in the suspense of it all. Dozens of pairs went down, and some made it all the way to the bottom and some didn't, one way or another. The day wore on, and so did the rescue folks.

Finally, there were only two contestants left. At present, there were two men at the top of the leader board who were tied for the lead, one from eastern Montana and the other all the way up from Utah. If neither of the final two contestants could best their time there'd be a run-off at the end. As it happened, just another one of those odd turns of fate I suppose, the final two contestants were the guy with the crazy birdhouse on skis and our very own Gil Carson. As it also happened, even though the guy with the birdhouse kept saying "cuckoo" all the time the day before, it turns out he wasn't completely nuts after all and scratched from the run at the last second, somewhat to the disappointment of those members of the crowd who enjoy a spectacle that also includes things blowing up and people taken to hospitals. And so, Gil would have the slope to himself.

Gil stood alone at the top of the slope, and through

binoculars you could see him clearly. He wore goggles and a headband, and his long blond hair blew out behind him like a scarf in the breeze. Standing on end beside him was a six-foot Radio Flyer, and it was an absolute beauty of an antique, and Gil had obviously put some work into it. Its red paint and glossy stained wood gleamed in the sun. Among the crowd here and there people shouted his name, cheering on the last hometown contestant who had a chance to win. When the time came, instead of having pushers give him a running start, Gil backed up about ten feet from the starting line and when the "go" came he tore down the runway with the sled held out beside him and flung himself on it and he was off!

By now the slope had been packed and packed again and was as hard as ice, which was perfect for his sled. He came down the first stretch of slope and you could hear his sled sing over the icy snow. He was going fast, very fast, at least as fast as any of the prior contestants as he neared the first boulder. He bounced along, he skidded sideways a bit, he dragged his left foot just a bit, like a rudder or something, and then he slid by the boulder missing it by inches and plummeted onward down the slope. When he passed us at midway I think we were all in shock at how fast he went by.

He was in a straight stretch now and continued to pick up speed, but the second boulder was almost right in front of him now and he was going way too fast. He was going so fast now that there was no way in the world he could ever hope to steer and...and then he was past the boulder, somehow, miraculously! We all started shouting then as he hit the last straightaway and crossed the finish line in a spume of snow and ice. He got off his sled and then stood below and raised his arm and we all went nuts with shouting.

And then we waited for the time-keeper to call in his time to the top of the slope, and we waited, everyone saying that surely his was the fastest run. It had to be. And then we heard Delmer's voice read out the time and it was true! Gil had won the day!

Then it was absolute pandemonium and we all slogged through the snow down to the finish line and Gil was mobbed. He was laughing and almost every-one else was too. His two nearest competitors came up and gave him a hug, and then later there was the award ceremony and Gil got the big trophy, not to mention the cash. It was a glorious day for both Gil and Dobbins, and the parties went on into the night, and wherever you happened to be, everyone was talking about Gil's Great Run. And so we would remember it always. We'd talk about it late at night and remember.

CHAPTER TWELVE:
A-VIKING

In the past tense I was a college professor, for quite a long time as it happens. My specialty was in medieval literature and languages, and my sub-specialty was in Norse studies. I bring this up only to point out that I once had a real job, and also because I wanted to tell you something about Vikings. The reason I want to, is because some people have completely misunderstood what it was to be a Viking. No, I'm not talking about the ravaging and invasions and swords and such, that's all pretty much true. However, you have to understand that being a Viking was as much about exploration and opportunity as anything else.

For one thing, most people think that a Viking was someone from Norway, and while that's largely true, there were actually Vikings from all over the place: Sweden, Denmark, Ireland and even Russia. The simple reason for this is that to go "a-Viking" merely means to leave the "viks" or fjords of one's home. And, the reason that most of them did so was because there really wasn't much going on at home to keep them there: heavy-handed kings, too many older brothers who got the farm, you're a bit low on food and shelter to make it through another Ice Age winter, and so on.

All I'm trying to say here is that if you really wanted to be a Viking you know what you'd do? You'd leave home and go looking for something else, something better.

So, as I understand it from other people, that's exactly what Einar and his wife Siggi did. They both grew up in Minnesota and Einar inherited the big farm from his father when he was just in his twenties and then he and Siggi got married and that was that. Einar and Siggi were high school sweethearts and when they got married and settled in on the big dairy farm they couldn't be happier, that is until the arrival of their daughter a year later.

Both of them were so happy they could bust, but their daughter became ill and then they lost her just two years after that. Einar and Siggi were devastated by this as you might imagine, and apparently their daughter's death haunted them in just about everything they saw and did. A day didn't go by when they'd see her there in the house stumbling around with her arms out and then laughing at this thing or that and trying to say she didn't like fried pike and so on. Every little thing just broke their hearts again and again.

There came a day when they were sitting around the kitchen table one cold night and Siggi said "I know this is going to sound crazy but I don't want to live in this house any longer. I can't stand it and I don't think I'll ever be happy again as long as we're living here."

Einar nodded and held her hand for a bit, and then he took her by the arm and they went to sit on the couch in the front room and they started to talk about what they might do. Later, Einar started talking to this person and then that one, and somebody said this and another said that, and he went and talked to some re-altors who said they'd keep an eye out for him, and the upshot of all this is that eventually they learned that there were cattle ranches for sale out in Montana, and hey, that wasn't so far away.

"The hockey's not so good there I understand," Einar said, but Siggi said it seemed like a good thing, as long as Einar thought he could handle cattle instead of dairy cows.

Einar laughed. "You kidding?! You don't even have to milk 'em!"

They had no problem getting a big advance from the bank on the sale of their place because there were sev-eral interested buyers, and so one summer they went on out west and started to look around. The way some people tell it is that they sort of shopped around, be-cause there were actually a few ranches up for sale and they wanted to be where they could settle down for good and all.

They took their time and looked at everything, and when they got to the ranch over by Dobbins they were absolutely sure and they bought the place. I guess that was some years back now, and what Kenna said Maude had told her was apparently true, because after a while Einar started buying more and more land to add onto what he already had, and I guess that's when he and Jack had their little to-do about a certain piece of property. But that wasn't the whole story, as I came to find out later. I'll try to remember to tell you about that later if I can remember.

74

CHAPTER THIRTEEN:
SHOOTING STARS

The other night was the Persid meteor shower, and one of the things that Joanie and I have discovered about living in Big Sky country is that there's a whole other view just looking up. The night skies here afford one with an unparalleled view of the heavens with no interference from the seven light bulbs that might still be on down in Dobbins, two miles below our place.

It's amazing to just sit out in lawn chairs, any time of year unless it's when it's crazy-cold, and just watch the stars. Sometimes we count satellites or planets or constellations. There we were, sitting out on the driveway in our lawn chairs, the dogs laying here and there, and Joanie had her telescope set up in case we wanted to look at something in particular, but tonight was the meteor shower. We watched them here and there just arc or shoot through our horizon and we'd shout and say "There!" and point, and once, just the once, we saw a fireball cross the celestial dome and fragment, right in front of us, breaking into red and orange and purple balls of flame like the grandest fireworks one can ever see and we said nothing for a few moments, perhaps reflecting on our smallness, just sitting there in awe because we'd both been looking right at it, and then we whooped with joy. You can never know when you'll see a shooting star. You can almost never be looking in the right direction and see it coming like you want to. They happen all the time and the only reason you think it's unusual is because you weren't looking in the right direction.

After Gil had won the big race almost a week now past, I went down to The Paper to see Chip and Jeff to see what stories they were working on about it for the next issue, and when I came in the door I saw Jeff busily typing away at his keyboard but Chip was just sort of poking at his, rather glum looking if I do say so. I was still in a pretty good mood about Gil winning the race and so I didn't really pay too much attention to Chip, but I did say "What's up guys?" and looked particularly at Chip.

Jeff paused in his work and looked up.

"Hey Al. Don't worry about him. That new guy took Jill on a date and he saw them and now he's love-lorn or something. I keep telling him that Jill's a big girl and can of course go out on dates whenever she likes, and that maybe ol' Don Jaun here is wasting his time thinking about it and had better start doing something instead."

Meanwhile, Chip looked at his computer screen and made a very decisive "thunk" with his index finger to the keyboard, looked up at me and then at Jeff with a look that, well, it wasn't particularly charitable I suppose, and then back at me.

"Hey Al. How's it going?'

I replied by saying it was all well and good with me, which of course was an abject lie, but that's what we're supposed to do socially, because nobody really wants to hear your problems it seems. And so I plunked myself down in a chair and that's when Walter of all people came through the door.

I had never seen Walter come into The Paper before, and now I think about it, I'm not sure I'd ever see him almost any time when he wasn't on duty, out on the street or the highway or the country roads somewhere. From the expression on Chip and Jeff's faces, I gathered that this was unusual for them as well. But the most disconcerting thing was the look on Walter's face. He looked, well, words like "ashen" and "grim" that you always hear just don't seem to say what I mean. He was those things, but tired too, you could see it in his eyes, and maybe even shocked in some way, and that was maybe most troubling of all. He carried a blue notebook in one hand, and once he had shut the door he took off his hat and found a chair to sit in and he hadn't said a single word yet. He looked at us one by one, tapping that notebook on his thigh as if thinking what he was going to say and hadn't decided yet. We looked back and waited. I had never seen him without his hat on. Never.

"It's Gil," he said, and he looked down at the floor for a moment. "A couple of people called me up. Said he hadn't been at the gas station for a couple of days maybe. The place hasn't opened I guess since maybe Monday. Somebody said they went to check on him in case he was sick or hurt and banged at the door and nobody answered, even though his truck was parked in the drive. They were worried maybe he'd hurt himself or something, so they gave me a call. I thought I'd better go see." Walter paused again and looked around a bit and ran a hand through his hair.

"So I did. Front door was locked but the back wasn't so I let myself in." And Walter looked at us again, one by one, and he was hurting now, you could see it. "I found him in the front room. He'd hung himself from a beam in there. Been dead maybe two days." And you could see it now and understand, that expression Walter had, the one that mixes anger and shock and grief all at once, the one that you never ever want to see.

The three of us were so stunned that we couldn't say anything for a while there, and then finally Jeff said "Oh God! How can he, I mean why would he... Oh God!"

And Chip was saying something too now, about how it couldn't be that it just couldn't be, and then Jeff was saying something and I put my head in my hands and cried a bit. After a while as if by some unseen command we all stood up at the same time and gathered around Walter and maybe we patted his shoulder or something and we probably said some other things too but I don't remember what they were. And then we stood and we looked out windows as if something were there, and we walked around the little room some more and then I think we sat again because that was all we could do. And there was nothing. There was no action or words or anything. We hung our heads. We sensed in some otherworldly way that you know things and can never say and knew it. Finally, Walter looked down at his hand with the notebook in it.

"He left this behind," Walter said, lifting his hand and stretching out his arm with the notebook in it, attempting to hand it off to no one in particular.

"Looks like he's been writing in it for some time. I read some of it. I wanted somebody to have it and know. I," and he paused, "I thought maybe it should go to his mother, but I read some of it you know?"

For reasons I will never really know, I put out my hand and received the notebook. I don't know why, I just did. And when I did Walter's shoulders sagged a bit, as if in release of some kind of burden, and then he straightened and put his hat back on.

"I have paperwork. I have to see his mother. I might also stop by at Simon and Theo's folks' places and say something too, I don't know yet. I have to go."

He looked at us again and we said things or nodded, I just don't really remember all the little bits of things very well is all. Walter turned then and opened the door and let himself out and it seemed as though the door closed very quietly behind him. And what was left then was the three of us, and Chip and Jeff were looking at me and then I remembered I was holding the notebook. We went and got chairs and pulled up to Jeff's desk and we sat. I held the notebook for a bit just looking at it, and then I looked up and Chip and Jeff were looking at me and so I opened it up and started turning the pages. Then I started to read aloud.

I guess most of us in town knew the story about how Gil had wanted to be an archaeologist and work in faraway and exotic places, and how his father had willed the gas station to him and then the showdown with his mother and all that, and in this little thin blue notebook the first pages were just photos and notes about various digs that were going on around the world and new discoveries of this thing and that, and Gil's exclamations about them.

And I flipped the pages more and then there was just

his writing in blue ballpoint about the gas station and more about how fed up he was and how stupid he felt to be running a gas station, and then I couldn't read anymore and I looked up and Chip and Jeff were just about in tears again, and I was too, and I handed the notebook to Chip and he read for awhile, about Gil's growing anger with the pointlessness of what he was doing and about how there had to be a way for him to get out and do what he'd always wanted to do and then Chip stopped too because there were only a couple more pages left and he didn't want to see and none of us did, but he handed the notebook off to Jeff and Jeff read aloud what was left.

And the upshot of what was left was, in very large letters now: "And this is it. I've won a sledding race and this is to be what I'll be remembered for in years to come. It's not enough. It was never enough." And that was all.

Jeff closed the notebook and held it in his lap and we all looked out the window at something I guess, but none of us knew what it was.

CHAPTER FOURTEEN:
MY BITTER HALF

The thing is, what I've come to see from just time to time, usually in that part of one's mind where things are less distracted because what you're doing at the moment is trying to concentrate and get a fencing staple into the fence post and you're having to try to get the blasted thing aligned just right because if you don't you're either going to mash your fingers again with the hammer or else mess up the nail and you re- alize you just put the one in your pocket for some stupid reason and that one is a bit longer on the one end than the other and so you're going to have to be careful or else it's a long walk back to the garage to get another and then you're wondering why you didn't bring your glasses with you and that's pretty much the only time you get to think about anything else it seems like.

So, what I'm thinking is, is that I just don't have time to think, but I know for certain that's not true because I'm only kind of working these days as compared to what I was doing before and so I guess that's not it but I wish it was because this whole thinking thing has changed for me in the past, oh, maybe a couple dozen months or so, just a tick on the clock I guess. So it's not really all that long but even so I'm just kind of getting the hang of it again okay? The thing is about this thinking about things is that I can't figure out what happened because I am pretty much the same as always I think, but Joanie is telling me I'm not and I don't get this because I have a pretty good idea of where and who I am and yet Joanie is always saying that I'm not it seems and then there's just the times like the fence post to think about it and usually I just mash my finger with the hammer and then I'm mad about that, and who wouldn't be?

And maybe you know by now that I have a hard time talking about anything that actually matters in this little life of ours, and so what I'm really trying to say here is that I've been mashing my thumb with the hammer for, oh, I don't know how long anymore, with Joanie, except I'm not talking about hammers and fence posts. Are we okay with this? Because if we aren't then you need to understand that I can't figure out how to talk about this, and you'll want to skip ahead to the chapters that have fishing or flowers or something in them.

So anyway, something falls into my head one morning and I have no idea where it came from. Maybe ideas are like those little meteorites that apparently shoot down through the atmosphere all the time. I read where you can lay out a sheet or something during the peak of these things and then in the morning go and find all these little, well, space things on your sheet. You ever do that? No, me either, because if we did then Grip and Tan would have been all over the sheet and I could just see us telling NASA we had something and then them coming all the way out to look and us saying "Well, Grip did look a little ill after that big bone yesterday." I'm just trying to say that I said to Joanie that we should go camping. Just get away. I don't know why I said that, and I don't know where the little meteorite of an idea came from. I thought it would be good. We always liked camping. Maybe we could just talk and enjoy ourselves with nothing else to do?

So we got everything packed up in Chuck's back bed and Grip and Tan were in the back seat and of course they had more room than usual because Finn wasn't there and I think Joanie noticed that, the extra space, and we headed off to a very nice little lake where we would spend a couple of days doing nothing but enjoying ourselves.

When we got there, we got the tent up in no time flat, because that's the way we are. You get there, get set up and now it's time to do what you got there for. We're good at it, a team you see, and we don't even say anything to one another when we set it up. We just do it from routine anymore. We just lay it out and poles here, poles there, one side working just in tune with other side, and bingo! We have our tent set up. We have a very nice tent, with a floor blanket for the dogs and cots for us, and then of course more pillows and such for the dogs because we don't want them to be in any way uncomfortable even if we are, and we got all settled. That was nice. That was fairly routine I think for us. "Us" was really all that mattered.

Of course, what we usually discover, especially Joanie who is a very busy person with her big online business, and then also myself because I can't figure out what

I'm supposed to be doing any more, is that after a couple of hours, or maybe less, we each of us start thinking what the heck should we be doing out here anyway? Should we take photos of the fungus , or determine if the tree overhanging the tent is a pine, spruce or cedar? Maybe the dogs would like another brisk hike around the lake? But usually, we think maybe we should sit back in our chairs like we're really relaxed and read our books and then every so often turn to one another and smile, and the smile of course says "This is very nice isn't it? Why don't we do this more often?" The truth is, I can't settle down like I used to and I get bored. That's probably why we always have enough wood sitting next to the fire-ring to last a week.

After a bit Joanie said. "The lake looks perfect. Will you get my kayak for me? I want to take a nice quiet paddle I think."

I pulled down her kayak from the rack I put on Chuck when we have our outings like this, and got her paddle and vest and then Joanie was set to go. Joanie is pretty savvy with kayaks and canoes, and pretty much anything else, but this time as she was getting in the kayak she must have just mis-stepped or something, because one moment she was halfway in the kayak and then the next it had rolled away and she was on her back in the lake.

Do you know what the German word *schadenfreude* means? It's a great word because it's one of those ones that describe something in a single word that takes us many words in English to express. I suppose an easy translation is: the feeling of joy at someone else's misfortune. Kind of harsh there I suppose, and I can't help but wonder about cultures that come up with easy words like that, but maybe it's simply linguistic efficiency. Anyway, the reason I laughed was not because of that. It wasn't.

Grip and Tan were right there with me and they laughed first. And laughter is contagious, you know. Everyone knows that. It's why when you get the giggles in church when you know you shouldn't be laughing and because the person next to you knows you shouldn't be laughing then they start laughing too. So Grip and Tan were laughing. They were! And they had huge grins on their faces: "Ha ha. Mom is so very wet. Ha! She didn't mean to do that I bet." Well, and that was very funny to hear them say that, and so, well, I kind of laughed some too.

I know you can already see the outcome of this. Joanie was not at all pleased about soaking herself and even less so about the three of us laughing at her expense. She righted herself with a choice imprecation and then waded back to shore. Her kayak continued to drift into the lake, and so I waded in to get it. That's when the push came in my back.

After I stood up in the lake I saw Joanie making her way back to the tent and I hauled the kayak to shore. I too made my way back to the tent. What followed was some awkward changing of clothing in complete silence. We returned to our lawn chairs and picked up books and sat in silence reading because how else can you read very well except in silence?

Later, in silence, I made a really nice dinner. The sun went down and the fire was going. We had a glass of wine. We started talking about the lake and oh, this wildflower, and had you ever seen ones with leaves that big before and no I never had. Dinner was going along very nicely on the coals and the dogs had already been fed and we were very pleased with everything right then, and there were a few sparks leaping up from the coals, a few stars on the eastern ridge just now appearing. It was beautiful. It's what we wanted.

I got our plates and said everything was ready, and we were really hungry by then, and that's when the first drops of rain came down. Not your little raindrops that you might sit and ignore, but big fat ones that will splash in your plate and send food into your face. We both looked up then and could see the clouds rolling in over the ridge. We filled our plates and got into the tent.

Except for having to repeatedly tell Grip and Tan that they'd already eaten, we had a nice meal in the tent. This was to be expected. Things happen when you're camping and it's never perfect. That's what camping is all about. What camping is about is being outdoors and doing without certain comforts and enjoying others. That's what it's about. And that's about when the wind got up.

It was starting to get dark and we needed to get things put away and of course make sure Grip and Tan had done what they needed to do before we locked ourselves in the tent. Raingear? Oh, that's in Chuck's back seat. Back in a minute. Why am I getting it? Why am I getting soaked again? I don't know, but I am. I return with raingear and wet clothing for my third change of the day. I am not very happy.

But, I grabbed what I could, ran back to the tent, sort of uselessly because there was no way I was going to get out of this particular rain without getting completely soaked, and once back inside I changed clothes yet again, to something slightly less wet than what I had on.

The dogs settled and we got into our sleeping bags.

And then the rain really started to come down. It came down so hard that we all got closer together in the middle, and then there was a leak in the middle that came down just right in the center of the tent. Just right in the center. Right in the center upon which everything depends. And what are you going to do? But Joanie was saying to do something and I didn't know what it was supposed to be, and so I got up and on hands and knees unzipped the tent flap and reached my arm out into the dark and the deluge to where I knew something was. I pulled in a pot from the cookware and sat it in the middle of the tent and the leak dripped perfectly into it. I smiled at Joanie in the lantern light, the sort of smile that says "How about that? I fixed it all up."

And then the tent collapsed on us.

CHAPTER FIFTEEN:
INSIDE INFORMATION AT THE BEAUTY PARLOR

After I left Kenna's place that day upon learning of the marital strife between her and Hollis I couldn't keep still, and being the nosey person that I am I wanted to find out what had happened, and besides these were my friends, and besides that I needed a haircut, so I called up Kenna near the end of the day and asked if she could get me in either early or late. Kenna, being the sort of person she is, had a pretty good idea of why I'd asked that and so she said, "Sure Al. Maybe I can get you in tomorrow right at the end of the day. Say five?"

When I got there the next day I pulled up to the curb and waited until it was five o'clock and I saw Kenna come up to the window of her shop and look out and she of course saw me there and I looked back and she put the "closed" sign in the window and then opened the door for me. I left Chuck and went inside. I said thanks and how you doin' and those kinds of things and what a nice summer it was so far and I went ahead and sat in the chair and instead of putting an apron on me Kenna pulled up a chair across from me and sat down.

"Well, go ahead," she said. "You already know every-thing I want to say to anybody, so if you want to say somethin' yourself go ahead."

I sort of looked at the floor for a bit then, and all I could manage was "I'm sorry Kenna. I don't want to pry. I guess I was surprised is all and maybe a little worried."

"'Bout who? Me or him?" she said, and then she leaned back in her chair and said "Sorry. I didn't mean that. It's just everbody's been wheedlin' away at me and I just don't want to talk about it is all."

"I can understand that," I said. "Maybe I'll just get that haircut if that's okay."

Kenna stood and started cutting my hair and she asked what was new, and that reminded me of our re-cent visit by Jack, and I told her all about that and also about those two columns I wrote and she said she'd read those and had known right away trouble was go-ing to come from it. That surprised me and I asked why.

"Those two have been feudin' as far back as most people around here can remember. Maude says they both showed up about the same time and I guess they both had pretty good bank accounts because they started buying up any land that was available, both of 'em. Didn't seem to matter what it was either, or so Maude says. Pasture land, water, rocks, mountains, whatever, they just bought what they wanted and I guess they've done alright by it. Anyway, she says that when they were on their buying spree that there was a chunk of land they both wanted. I guess there's a few places here and there where their property runs up against each other's, which doesn't surprise me owing to them owning pretty much the whole county between the two of them. So they had some sort of spat about it and one of them got it and the other didn't and they've been feudin' ever since. Even their hired hands don't hang out with one another. You'll see 'em down at The Office, one bunch over by the bar and the other bunch hangin' over by the pool table, and as far as I know there's never been any trouble between the two crews, but they don't even talk to one another if you can believe it! I don't know anything about the whole hay bale thing, but it doesn't surprise me either. Once I had Einar in here gettin' his hair cut and Jack walks in and sees who's here and he just turns and walks right back out the door. They'll disagree about what color the sky is. You ever see Einar with a hat on? I mean, ever? You ever see Jack without one? Doesn't matter what it is, they'll be feudin' over that too!"

And now Kenna was getting a bit worked up for some reason I didn't quite understand, and I was suddenly remembering yesterday's lopping off of hair when I walked in, but I reassured myself that there's very little chance of anyone, no matter their mood, altering my hair very much in a way that might make it somehow worse than it is. Kenna went on, both snipping and talking.

"And the damn thing is," she said with some emphasis, "the damn thing is, they won't even talk to one another! They just don't even bother to try to listen, and they could! I bet you if they just sat down and had a beer and talked for a bit then they'd make things right because they're both decent guys from what I hear, and they just don't even want to do that even!"

Kenna stopped snipping then, and she didn't start back up. I wasn't facing the mirror so I couldn't see why she stopped. I swiveled around to look at her and she was crying. Kenna took her hand away from her mouth then, and rubbed an eye with a fist.

"It's just that he won't talk anymore Al. He just kind of stopped or something and it's like I lost him or something, but it was more like he just went away or something. He just kind of stopped. I talked to him and some days he seems like everything's okay and then other days it's like he's somewhere else. I tried to get him to come back and he said he would and he didn't and I got so mad I told him to get out and never come back and I was so mad."

I listened to this with just about half my head because there was something here that was going on with me past present or future that was nagging at me as if I'd just been reminded of it for the first time in a long time and the rest of what was going on inside my head was someplace else like it seems to be and I think it was memory or maybe understanding or maybe that thing called empathy which I only half remember, but I think I was nodding my head throughout all of what Kenna was saying, either because I knew what she meant or because it was somehow reminding me of something else.

I don't really know any longer why I think the way I do, where something makes me think of something else and then that thought goes down some badger hole and comes back up in a rabbit hole or whatever it is that's going on, but I had some thoughts about what Kenna was saying and whether or not I meant to say them to her or someone else I said "He got those scars somewhere, you know. He showed me once I think. I know you've seen them better than anyone ever has."

Kenna went over to the wall then, where her audience usually sat, and found a chair.

"Yeah. I've seen 'em. War Hero you know? Been all over. He doesn't talk about it, but he's got this little box out in the garage where he keeps all his medals and I've seen 'em. He's got a lot of them. Ever tell you he's got a Service Star and all? I think they gave up on the Purple Hearts after a while. Once I came out there when he was doing something with the truck and he was lookin' at 'em. He was sad was all. I asked him if he'd show me and all he did was just shut the box."

I nodded and looked at her, thinking my muddled thoughts, and I got up and took off the apron and Kenna said she wasn't done and I turned around and looked in the mirror and it seemed as though I hadn't done so for quite some time and I said it's fine. I'm okay.

And then, when I was headed to the door Kenna said "I just want the idiot to come back and talk. That's all. That's all we need, but he just won't and when I threw him out I thought the gristle-brain would figure it out and come back. I just want him back the way he was."

I stood at the door, and all I could say was "I'll get him. No worries about that. But Joanie's waiting for me. I have to go."

I made my way out, not thinking at all if Joanie was really waiting for me or not.

And I walked out trying to remember what it was, past present and future, just something that wouldn't let me alone. It was something I needed to say, or do, to someone or for someone, or maybe even more than one person, but I couldn't remember. It was all jumbled up somehow, just like always.

CHAPTER SIXTEEN:
AN UNEXPECTED MEETING WITH THE GODS OF THE UPPER AIRS

Dobbins does not have a public park. This is of course entirely logical when you live in Montana. I mean, why in the world would you want some tiny little place to be set aside where you can go and sit and then have someone who made the park tell you all the things you can't do while you're there? We saw this sort of thing when we were in Oregon I'm afraid, where park rules told you that essentially you'd better sit at a picnic table and very quietly have a conversation about philosophy or something, and don't you be doing anything else. In Oregon there are no-smoking signs in parks, and I'm not kidding, because who knows which way the wind might blow at any second and probably kill someone else over several decades? Thankfully, this is Montana and there are no rules. Well, maybe some.

However, there is, what maybe, once upon a time, might have been a train station. I haven't ever asked anyone, but it's just along the tracks of the freight rail that runs just outside of town which never stops here, and here and there are old foundations of something, something that is no longer here. What is here, however, is an old picnic table and ancient willows, and when I need to be alone I come here with The Paper and my coffee and Chuck parks under his favorite tree and I sit at the table and read, or just watch the birds or something. I have this bad feeling that I'm just trying to find somewhere to be out of the house.

I seem to sit here quite a lot anymore when I have nothing to do and my mind wanders to wherever it has to go I suppose. Sometimes I think about my past life as a college professor, and sometimes I miss it. I used to teach a mythology class on a regular basis and it was always full. People love the old stories about gods and goddesses and the crazy things they'd do, and heroes who either defied them or got assistance from them, and love stories and tragedies of course. They're the oldest stories, and maybe because of that, the best ones too, however they might go.

So, there I was, not doing much of anything, when who should come by on their bikes, laughing at one another about this and that, but Morningstar Jackson and Thor Einarson. Sitting there watching them pedal up the dirt road to where I sat you could tell they were best friends. They had an easy manner about them-selves and they laughed and smiled and pushed at each other even while on their bikes. It made me smile to watch them. I thought, here they come: the God of Thunder and Lightning and the Goddess of Dawn. I laughed a bit at that I think.

Oooh boy, now there was a marriage quite literally made in the heavens that maybe shouldn't have been. Or, I don't know, I mused, maybe not. There'd be ol' Thor out storming all night long and then the Goddess of Dawn, out of bed early of course, would see him come home exhausted and say "All done for the night dear? Mind if I get to work and clean things up a bit?" You know, the woman's touch and all that, making things right again.

I think that was about when it occurred to me that this wasn't just two kids I was seeing, but rather the offspring of the Jacksons and the Einarsons, who had been feuding about something as stupid as hay bales, apparently for many years now, and who of course were the two most powerful families for four-hundred miles. I had a feeling I might just be seeing a tragedy playing out in front of me, and I also had a pretty strong feeling that neither Jack nor Einar had any idea about this friendship.

The two of them finally took their attention away from one another long enough to see me looking up at them and Morningstar veered in my direction and of course Thor did too, because they were clearly in each other's orbit the whole time.

"Hi Mr. Smith," Thor said formally, skidding to a stop, but with still an almost breathless smile on his face from whatever he and Morningstar had been laughing about.

"Hi Al," said Morningstar, in completely proper Montana greeting to an elder. "How's Chuck?"

"He's doing quite well," I said, "thanks to you."

"Dad loved your piece in the newspaper about his hay bales," Thor added. "He's got it framed in his study!"

"Oh," I said. "Does he? Um, well, that's good I think."

I studied them a moment and said "Looks like you two are having a fine old time. What's the occasion?"

"It's after school!" Thor said. "We don't get picked up by our parents for two hours after school."

"Really? How come?"

"So we can ride our bikes together," Morningstar said, and kind of cocked her head at me in that look I'd seen before, like she was studying why I was so dense, or maybe just weighing me in some way I couldn't understand.

"Oh," I said, "well that's real nice that your parents give you some time together to go around and all. That's really nice."

Thor dipped his head a bit, and I could tell I'd just stepped into something they didn't want to talk about, but Morningstar looked at Thor and said "It's okay. He's alright."

And I guess she meant me, because she turned and said "You know. Our folks don't like each other. Everyone knows. So we told them we stay late at school so we can go out and ride."

I looked back and forth at them. "Hmmm, that's kind of risky don't you think?"

"I'm supposed to be at Chess Club," Thor said and laughed. "I'm really lousy at chess!"

Morningstar smiled her ten-thousand-dollar smile and said, with a flick of her ponytail, "I'm studying for college exams, but I finish pretty fast. Then we can go riding, see?"

I saw.

Oooh boy, I thought, I hoped they'd never get caught doing so or you could pretty much bet they'd never be allowed to see one another again. I couldn't help but ask.

"I'll assume that your biking forays are all on the down-low, right? I mean, you wouldn't want your folks finding out right?"

"Dad'd probably send me to camp or something," Thor said, no smile now on his face.

"I have it all figured out," Morningstar said, and smiled brightly once again.

I looked again at them, back and forth.

"So, what's going to happen when they find out?"

Thor had a stricken look, as though this might be the end of all his happiness if that happened.

"Don't worry," I said. "I'm not going to tell." I had some coffee then. "It's not mine to tell, and I wouldn't if it were."

Thor, relieved, straightened a bit and then looked to Morningstar, his light in whatever that window was where it was supposed to break or something.

"See? I told you he was okay," Morningstar said, and beamed at Thor. Her smile meant everything to him, I could tell.

And I saw that their hands wanted to touch, just for an instant, but they didn't. They each just slightly fluttered like something I'd seen before. Maybe it was leaves, the ones in spring that are just alive and so full of themselves they twist and turn to show themselves off dancing together in rhythm to the breeze, or maybe blades of grass speaking to one another and how they rub up against one another spreading the news of the earth that they cover, sharing everything together always, or maybe how two little stones thrown in the pond each ripple out but maybe quite not meet, or the two halves of the moon, grey and white, give each other their completeness. I'd seen it before, I'm sure of it. I just can't remember where. It's somewhere. Past present future. I know it. I've seen, saw, seeing it.

I put my head down because I knew this story and you do too.

"You're going to get caught eventually," I said, my very wet blanket coming out now, and I don't know why I just couldn't keep my mouth shut for once.

Why just say that and spoil their time together? I have no idea. I think maybe I just wanted it to be and saw that it couldn't, or maybe I just wanted a better plan or something. I don't know, but I shouldn't have said that.

Morningstar looked at me again, and then smiled once again.

"No we won't. I have it figured, just like I said. It's how we're here right now. I have everything figured out."

I looked up at the willow then, weeping of course, and said "I know how smart you are Morningstar, but can you tell me how the light shines in the Halls of Shambala?"

I looked back down and Morningstar had a very puzzled look on her face. At least I could ask one question that she couldn't answer. I was glad I guess for flummoxing a thirteen-year-old, because I didn't have any answers either. What would you say?

CHAPTER SEVENTEEN:
BUSTED UP

I feel like telling you about something, but I can't imagine why. I mean, it doesn't have any relevance to what I've been telling you about these other things. I don't know. I'm just trying to say something here and I don't know what it is until I've said it.

One summer morning Chuck and I went fishing, and everything went pretty much the way it always does. You know? It was a drive in the dark, and Chuck and I said this and that and I said where are we going and Chuck said what do you feel like and I said this that and the other would be fine, but it was his preference this morning though it wasn't morning yet, and Chuck said he knew just the place and so we went quite a bit further out than we usually do on our fishing jaunts because that's what he wanted and that's okay with me.

We got where we got and I could tell Chuck was feeling a bit smug about all this because we hadn't come here in quite a while and he said I bet the water here is just perfect right now because I remember last year you said it was this same week a year ago, and I marveled at his memory for things like that. I patted his dashboard. Good ol' Chuck. He always looked out for me, no matter what. He parked in the shade because he knew it would be hot later, even in just a couple of hours, and I got out and struggled into waders and boots and vest and strung my rod and said my good-byes.

I made my way down to the river. It wasn't too far, just a while of walking in the almost-dark where everything slips away. I'd tell you about the walk, but now I was on the river.

This place, it really doesn't matter where it is, is all places all at once, because you can see it's never at rest, the water going by. It's the river. It's always past present future, all the time all at once, coming down from somewhere, moving by me in the here-and-now, and then already someplace else even in the present tense, you see? It's always there and here and been and gone all the time. You see? And here I don't worry about how my head has been scrambled. Why would I? There's nothing else but the river.

I cast and I cast. My little fly moved across the waters, and it is plural, because there are different waters all making up the one. There are the slow and the quick and the ones that eddy out into something or not. There are the ones that you may stand in, and those that you may not, not in this life. There is much to see and much to not see, and so there are choices. Where would I like to be? What will be my next cast? Where will it come from and why?

And, there was this very nice rock, just a rock you understand, where I wanted to be next for whatever reasons there might be. I waded over to it, a little sideways and a little further into the torrent, and I stood on the rock. Ha! But not for long, because that's when one boot gave way and the other followed and I slammed down hard onto another rock, and then I got carried away, keeping my head in the air as best I could, and luckily I slammed into a log against yet another rock in the river, or that might have been that. I dragged myself upright as best I could.

My leg hurt like hell, but it wasn't broken. I stood on it and tried to turn, ever so slowly, back to the bank. The water was shallower here where I'd been swept to, so I could likely get back to dry ground. My leg hurt a lot. I made it back to the bank slipping only once, but I had to say certain words over and over again to do so, like some very bad lecture. On dry ground, I found a good dead branch and used it as a crutch. I made my way back to Chuck, maybe fifty yards away. It took thirty minutes but felt like a month.

When I got back I sat in Chuck's back bed and groaned a while and Chuck worried, and ten minutes later I had gotten my boots off, and then more slowly my waders, but only with quite a bit of shouting about something, I don't remember what, something maybe about what God does when I don't understand very well, or something like that. My leg had now swelled so much that my jeans hurt, and I couldn't get them down over my right leg, and so I got the tiny pair of scissors from my fly vest and started to slowly cut down through my jeans, from the knee down on my right leg. That took a good twenty minutes or so, but it was worth it. I could now see my leg, already purple, and knew I had broken a blood vessel if not my leg. My foot was numb, and looked like something that belonged to Sasquatch. It was swollen to almost twice its normal size. I cut off the sock as best I could, because I couldn't reach down very far because I thought I might pass out if I did so for very long.

Eventually, I was as ready to go as I could be, and hopping on one leg I closed the tailgate and hopped to the door and then slid myself in, to the middle of the seat. There was no way I'd be using my right leg, so the left it would have to be. I told Chuck to go as slow as he could until we got to the main road, and then kind of easy from there on. Two hours later, we pulled into the driveway.

Thankfully, I saw Joanie was sitting in her car in the driveway, and so I wouldn't have to try to yell up at the house, because Chuck had no horn. He never needed one before and so it never bothered me.

Because I was in the middle of the seat I could easily roll down the right window and said to Joanie "I'm hurt. I need some help."

I saw Grip in the back seat, and he was panting for some reason.

Joanie said through the window without turning in my direction "Help me! I can't get up! Grip saw a squirrel and he ran and his leash caught me and took me down. I can't move! I barely got back in the car!"

Oh God. I panicked.

Now, just for a moment if you can, panic with me. My wife is hurt and in distress, but I'm just about pretty much immobile myself. What do you do? Yes, that's right. Whatever you have to.

Because I was mostly in the middle of Chuck's bench seat I figured the easiest thing to do was go out the right-hand door, so I slid myself over a bit and tried not to move my right leg. I got the door open and then lifted my leg out with both arms and swiveled enough to look at Joanie.

"I'll be right there. I hurt my leg. Give me a minute."

I hauled myself up onto the door and then hopped over to Joanie's car and opened the back so Grip could get out, and he ran around barking like mad until I sent him up to the porch to wait. I opened Joanie's door and hopped back out of the way. She looked at my cut-away jeans and my blackened leg.

"Holy cow, what happened to you?!"

"I fell off a rock but my fall was broken by another rock, and I am here today because God saw fit to put a tree in the river in my path."

I paused, with pain on my face that Joanie couldn't have seen because she hurt so much, and couldn't even turn her head very much.

"I need some sort of crutch before I can try to get you out. Give me a couple of minutes."

I could see bruising on the left side of her face and her left hand and arm. I turned and hopped toward the garage, each jolt producing a very limited number of words. Actually, it was just the same one. Luckily, there was a garden rake propped by the door, which I got and tested out. Not bad. Better than putting any weight on my leg or falling down. I made my way back to Joanie. Then we had to figure out what to do.

"Where are you hurt?"

"Pretty much all over," Joanie said. "Worse on my left side, but I've thrown out my back."

"Think you can get out of the car? Maybe we should call Delmer and get some help?"

"No!" Joanie said. "I don't want anyone to see me like this."

"Think you can at least get out? I mean, there's no way I can help a whole lot with one leg and one arm."

"Wish we had two wheelchairs," she said.

I opened the car door and Joanie tried to very slowly move sideways and got one leg out.

"Now what? My back is gone."

"Maybe grab the steering wheel and try to pull your-self up a bit, and then I can get an arm on you?"

This, however, produced a piercing scream from Joanie, but she did manage to get both feet out the door. The next piercing scream resulted in her hanging onto the car door with both feet on the ground, but bent over like she had a tractor on her back.

I'll spare you a bit of what happened next and just say that twenty minutes later we managed to get up the front porch steps and get inside. Joanie did this by screaming quite a lot as I inched her up the steps, and I did this by making heroic hops up each step until I reached the top, gripping the front door, and swinging myself inside with the garden rake in one hand.

Grip had watched all this of course, with me and Joanie shouting for him to please, please get out of the way, and when we got the front door open, there was Tan to greet us and her brother and Joanie and I stood as still as we could and said things like "Go play! Go play! No! Don't touch me, okay?!" Both Grip and Tan looked us over with some concern, but hey! There's five acres to run on. So they did. Thankfully.

I got Joanie as far as the living room couch and she got her feet up with only a couple more screams. I hopped to the bedroom and got her a pillow, then did a sort of limp-and-drag of a chair over to where Joanie was. I sat and we looked at each other. We were pretty busted up. I slid the chair closer and lifted Joanie's shirt a bit so I could see. Her whole left side was a bruise.

"Holy smokes," I said.

"Now what?" Joanie said.

That was a good question. Here in Dobbins and the surrounding enormous county we practice socialized medicine. That is, if somebody found you lying in your yard with a broken leg they might be sociable enough to go get a few other folks and lift you onto a blanket. After you'd passed out from that, they might put you in the back of a truck and make the hours-long drive over to where they actually have a hospital, or even a doctor, and hopefully you'd keep passing out along the way. Of course, during fire season you could pretty much count on the crews having medical personnel with them, and if you did it just right with a chainsaw on your truck seat and soot all over your face they'd patch you up pretty quick and send you on your way.

Yep, that was a good question.

"We have ibuprofen," I said.

"I'll split the bottle with you."

Now here's the thing, and maybe this is why I'm telling you about all this in the first place, but you'd kind of like to think that this was going to be one of those stories where Joanie and I re-learned how to trust and rely on one another and that we sort of pulled together in hard times and made it because of that, and of course were all the closer as a result. Nope. That's not what happened.

Maybe it was because we both hurt. Or maybe we were mad because it was summer. In winter, of course, we'd have had eight good months to look after one another and how are you doing today and can I get you a cup of tea and oh no don't get up I've got it. But, it was summer, and maybe that was it. This is your only chance to actually live here and you can't because you're busted up. And if you miss any of summer, for whatever reasons, you're going to regret it later.

I think this all started out on my part because neither one of us knows what the other really does on a daily basis, you know, like routines that we each just sort of take for granted all the time. This started that evening when Joanie told me it was time to feed the dogs. I had no idea what they ate, but I did know they had particular allergies and so you had to be careful. The way this went was Joanie on her back in the front room, me in the kitchen trying to hear, me hopping into the front room with the garden rake for further instructions, then me hopping back to the kitchen and then me hopping back to the front room and then the kitchen because I didn't catch that last thing she said.

And then it was time for making dinner. Guess who did that? And for the next three days. Know why? You have one leg! You win! You have one leg and so are at least quasi-mobile.

"I'm making goulash. I don't want to hear anything about that. It has all the food groups or pyramids or whatever they are these days in it, and it's served with red wine."

Later, after six days when Joanie could stand, she looked out the window: "What happened to the yard? The grass is two-feet high!"

"Missed it this last week you know, and we had rain."

Before Joanie could stand again then I was on-call. I tried to be good. In time I got a bit tired, or something, and then I did things grudgingly. Meanwhile, we'd sit in the front room watching the stupid TV which we only ever watch in the winter and gritting our teeth because it was summer. We weren't happy. We hadn't been happy together for quite some little time, and now we were unhappier.

This is another one of those places where I think I'm telling you when this happened, but I can't be sure. I am thinking thought will think that this is behind us. It could be in front, or the middle, I can't remember. I don't know. I want things to be better between us. I am trying to think in future tense, and what I want.

CHAPTER EIGHTEEN:
DUTY CALLS

I guess I've known Walter a little over two years now, though I've never actually known him. I mean, we don't meet socially or anything, and I've never met his wife Veronica either. I've seen them all of course, both of them and the triplets, lots of times, it's a really small town, but I guess I don't know anything about Walter and Veronica. Joanie and I may have said hello in the Safeway once or twice, but that's about all. Not much.

I have never in my life heard Walter laugh, but that doesn't mean a whole lot. I only see him when he's on duty, which seems pretty much all of the time, because he's all we've got around here for law enforcement. I wouldn't say that Walter is a humorless person, because I have seen Veronica here and there, chatting with people, and she always seems to be laughing, and so I can't imagine how someone like that would end up with a very un-laughing kind of person. Do you know what I mean? It's just that when I see Walter, and I suppose most other people too, he's always on duty, and I know for certain that he takes this very seriously.

I think I should also say that Walter is in no way some sort of Barney Fife who has been given authority and likes to lord it over others. No, that's not him at all. I've seen him dress down tourists and townies alike, sure, and have been on the undressed part of that a couple of times myself. I've also seen him talk to tourists in the summer and also during hunting season and give them directions and he tells them where the nearest cabins for rent might be and he gets his hand shaken quite a bit from grateful passers-through.

I also know that Walter cares about the folks in this county, because I've heard a dozen stories about how he helped fix this and that, and how he could have run in ol' so-and-so but didn't and instead really gave him a talking to because who would be feeding the family if he was in lockup, or when someone was rolled over in the ditch in heavy snow and Walter, always on duty, just happened to see a tire poking out of a drift and saved someone's life, and on and on.

But Walter is always on duty. I've never seen him otherwise, even at the Safeway with Veronica and the triplets in his immediate presence, he's still got his uniform on and I've only seen him once, just that time at The Paper when he came to tell us about Gil, that he didn't have his hat on. And when you have your hat on, I'm pretty much sure everyone knows what I'm talking about, because then you're on duty, right? I mean, you don't just wear *that* hat to shade your eyes.

And I don't know about this whole "on duty" thing and what it might do to a person. I know that people like firefighters and air-traffic controllers get kind of short shifts because what they do takes a lot out of them, and I know that I'm always, always respectful to nurses if I ever meet them, because you just have no idea what sorts of things they see day in and day out and what sorts of folks they have to put up with too. Besides, you don't ever want to make one mad anyway, because next thing you know you've got lemonade in your IV.

So, all I'm trying to say here in my usual not very clear way is that I never understood Walter. Not even a bit beyond what anyone could see of him. Not until that day in summer when I was just warming my hands over my to-go cup of coffee and sitting on The Bench outside of Del's. That's when Walter came up and I didn't even see him because I was staring out in space, thinking about me and Joanie and what was wrong, and why I couldn't think, or maybe I wasn't much thinking which happens you know, and that's when Walter came along and sat on The Bench, right where I was sitting.

And The Bench isn't like a very big bench or anything. It's the sort of bench that if you ever wanted to experiment with what personal space means to people you'd have a little clipboard with you and you'd see someone sit down on The Bench and then you'd come and sit down on it yourself, you know, all casual and everything, just to see how many seconds it took for the other person to get off it, and then you'd check a little box in your anthropology experiment and say to yourself, yep, just about six seconds to make somebody else uncomfortable, and put your pencil behind your ear. Besides, hardly anyone sits on this bench except me, and that's partly why I write about it in capital letters, because it's kind of mine.

So Walter just plunks himself down and says "Hey Al," and starts taking off a boot and says he's got something in there, and he wrestles with it for a bit and then holds his boot up and nothing comes out of it, and he's looking at it like it's some sort of trick or something because there's nothing coming out of it, and he's shaking the darn boot. He keeps shaking it and then, I don't know, I suppose he becomes resolved to the idea that there's actually nothing in his boot, and he sighs, I mean like one of those sighs that Shakespeare once intended for a huge crowd to hear, and he starts to put his boot back on.

"Boot bothering you?" I asked.

"Something," he said.

And then he looked up and we happened, for just that damndest moment, to be looking at each other's eyes. The problem with me these days is that I just don't want that to happen, because that's when you actually see people, you know, really see them, and holy moley I don't know how much I've got left in me to actually see people again. I really don't think I have it in me. But there it was: it was in his eyes. I saw it and couldn't miss it. I'd seen that look. I'd seen it in Hollis. I'd seen it in the mirror, back when I once looked in a mirror, and I don't look anymore, but I knew it. It was that look that I can't face anymore. My hand itched to put on Walter's shoulder, but I didn't.

This world, this world of ours, so full of very much everything, so very many things that you'll never know or see or experience, it's so far beyond my own little understanding that I have grown to know that whenever something just fires in my head that was just as it was supposed to be, I'm pretty much sure that I didn't have anything to do with it, because really, how could you, with so much else there? There's always so much else there that it's just hard to think most days.

"Gil?" I said.

Walter did not look up. He looked at his offending boot. He unlaced it and took it off and held it up and shook it again. He put it back on and relaced it and then he stood.

"I have to go," he said. He made something like a smile and said "Duty calls."

Oh God. Please don't do this to me again, because you know that I can't fix anyone and make them better, and you know that I'm the one who needs repair. You know? I just can't.

Chapter Nineteen:
Immunity

When I was a kid, I went through a series of mishaps one after another that took me to the doctor's office and even the emergency room. Big surprise, I know. Twice, Dr. Gildner came to our home to administer to me, and yes, they still did that back in those days and weren't so very busy and in love with their offices. Oh, I had all sorts of interesting things happen to me: burnt some poison ivy that got in my eyes, discovered I had some really ironic allergies, and even managed to get the rabies series shots, in the stomach back then, first and maybe only to do so in my little town.

Mom and Dad of course simply wrote this off as enthusiasm and "bad luck" and such. I mean, I had a raccoon as a pet when I was ten, and so really what could happen to me, and he slept on the bed and I'd let him out the window at night for a few hours. He'd come back in before dawn and curl up on the bed, and I never asked him what he'd been doing. Probably stuff that might get him sent to a raccoon emergency room. I only learned as an adult that they could have really nasty diseases and even people could get them.

I had a lot of really neat scars by the time I was

twelve, mostly on my hands, like where the muskrat bit me and then of course that was when I got the rabies shots. I had a really nice scar, and still do, on the back of my head where I misjudged a jump into the town swimming pool and cracked my head unconscious on the concrete and was saved by a school-mate from drowning.

I have just about stepped on Cottonmouths and Rattlesnakes maybe a dozen times, but never been bitten. My big brother, who's a minister to a large congregation, has never asked me to be a guest speaker because, you know, he's already good at that sort of thing, but I bet for sure I could bring around a couple of sinners here and there with how God has looked after me. Particularly with those serpents.

That summer when I worked deconstruction and the giant plate-glass window exploded on me and fell on my foot, and then at the emergency room they were able to dig around and get most of it out, but for the next ten years or so another piece of glass would surface and I'd get the tweezers and pull it out of my foot, every so often, maybe once each year for a while there, I think after that I thought I was done with being hurt. I was wrong of course.

Once, my high school girlfriend and I were driving back from a dance at another little, tiny town in Nebraska, along the gravel roads that make up everything except I-80, and the sky suddenly blackened like something out of a nightmare, black and purple, and a tornado swept up behind us and lightning blasted down all around us, sending plumes of plowed ground into the sky and my little car swayed in the wind and I tried to drive as fast as I could, trying vainly to remember if tornadoes travel south-west/ north-east, or was it the other way around and should I turn left or right?

But I have to tell you, that when the killer came to my little school and walked in, seemingly unnoticed, wearing body armor and carrying multiple anti-personnel weapons and many died in just a few moments, just tick-tick-tick-tick-tick-tick-tick-tick-tick and nine were dead including my best friend, and I screamed and screamed and got my students out from next door, then that of course was when I thought I was all done. You know, with trauma. You know, just see if you can deal with that one for a bit. The world is all done with me now. It's given me its best shot, so to speak.

And I remember my Mom and Dad looking at me one night after having gotten the rabies shots in the stomach again and the screaming and holding me to the bed and of course yet another tetanus shot, and Dad said "Look at it this way: You're pretty much immune to anything right now. I bet if you fell off a cliff you'd bounce right back up like The Abominable Snowman on Rudolph."

My Mom gave Dad a look which he saw.

"But, you know, don't test that out, because God doesn't care for you to do that sort of thing, you know, like jumping off the roof with Tom and those army surplus weather balloons."

Mom was still a little sore about her squashed juniper bushes after that one.

But you see, I've remembered all that, and after the shooting, many months later and for whatever reasons, I began to feel immune to any other trauma, or maybe just shut out anyone else's, and only had to just deal with the one. Just like Mom and Dad said, I'm immune now. What can possibly hurt me now, after that?

After the big sled race, Anders did not in fact go home to Minnesota and neither did his brother, who was apparently okay after his crash on the slope, and instead they stayed on somewhere, living in their fifth-wheel. From time to time you would see them walking around town or at the Safeway getting groceries, and they were always quite noticeable, especially Anders who was quite tall and blond and probably what I'm guessing some of the women in town would describe as rakishly handsome if I'd bothered to ask them.

I happened to be getting my hair cut at Kenna's one morning and I mentioned this fact to her.

She said, "Oh Yeah. He's still here because of Jill. I think they've been goin' out a bit now, maybe the past couple of weeks or so."

I thought a bit then about Chip, and said "So I guess it's true. Chip has some competition."

"I think they say 'game, set and match' in tennis, Al," Kenna said with a grin.

"That serious then?" I asked.

"I think they went over to the Wal-Mart in Butte to see if they had shirts where both people can fit inside them."

I laughed at the joke, but I couldn't help but think of poor Chip. I knew he really liked Jill, and so that had to be hard on him.

Of course the problem I have is that when I hear about anyone else's problems then for the most part I simply say the right things as best I can and file that somewhere in my head where I don't have to actually feel them. If I didn't, then I'd likely be a bucket of tears almost every day and I have a hard enough time functioning and pretending "I'm here" as it is. You see, I'm immune to trauma now. Got it? That's why I moved here.

Past present future, I know I've said this somewhere along the line, and it's just scrambled in a way that I can't make sense of, and I'm sorry about that. I mention this only because the next thing I want to say is about when Chuck and I went out fishing one morning and I have no idea how that follows on anything I've said so far. Okay?

Chuck and I are going fishing. Yes! This is a wonderful thing because the river is there, and the trees and the flowers and of course the fish and the mountains, and I don't even have to drive because Chuck takes care of that. Good ol' Chuck. I just drink my coffee and daydream about this and that and then eventually, wherever it is he's decided to go, then there we are. How nice is that? It's very relaxing, let me tell you.

The beauty of Chuck doing the driving is that I get to look at the scenery along the way, and also because I'm not paying attention to where we're going and am just sort of a tourist at the Chuck Guide Service, I am often surprised at where we end up. Sometimes I end up saying "Wow, Chuck! That was a great choice this morning," and other times "Really? Here?" But it's always okay. Chuck knows me and he tends on average to be very common-sense about things, you know, being a machine and all.

When I stopped daydreaming there for a bit and

looked out the windshield I was a little confused as to where we were until I remembered that this was the way up to one of the little alpine lakes, way up, where there was a beautiful stream coming out of it which was just full of little brook trout which were so fun to fool and then let go.

"Good choice, Chuck," I said, and patted the dashboard. "This should be good."

We bounced over washboard roads and snaked around boulders which stuck out in the way to get to the lake and ducked once under a recent dead-fall, but no big deal. This is how it always goes. But what I didn't expect, no not at all, was to find Jill and Anders of all people on this road, sitting on the tailgate of Jill's pickup.

This was unusual in the extreme. First, to find anyone you knew out in the mountains, anywhere in our enormous county, let alone the larger state, and then of all people Jill and Anders. I hadn't even known Anders was still here now that it was summer. I guess what Kenna said was true: it was pretty serious.

Chuck, being the observant one of us, and also probably the most gregarious, rolled to a stop just behind Jill's truck.

I got out and said "Hey you two, small world huh?"

"Hey Al!" Jill said jumping up off her truck bed. "I hoped that was Chuck I saw coming up the last switch-back! This is Anders, remember?"

"How could I forget?" I said as Anders came up and I thought we were going to shake hands but I got bear-hugged instead. What is it with these people who grow up in cold climates anyway?

"We actually ran out of gas," Anders said, "and if I had been driving I might have lied about that to Jill, you know, for just a little while, while we enjoyed the splendor of nature for a bit," and he smiled.

I did too.

Jill laughed and said "But I was driving, and my fuel gauge still says half-full, so something screwy is going on with my truck."

"No worries," I said as I got the five-gallon can of gas from Chuck's back bed, which most of us have on hand, just in case.

I poured it into Jill's truck and said "Want me to follow you down, just in case it's something else?"

Jill said no, because it was all downhill anyway all the way back to Dobbins, and she imagined I was here for fishing.

"Got that right," I said. "Chuck's taking me up to a nice little lake..."

And that's when a really beat-up ol' truck came into view, in a place where only I should have been at this time of morning, let alone having run into Jill and Anders. Small world, I guess.

But then the truck slowed, some ways still up the road, and I saw. There were Elk antlers sticking up in the back of the truck, badly covered by a tarp but I guess as best they could be. There was a man sitting in the back of the truck as well.

The truck came closer then, and Anders sat back down on the tailgate of Jill's truck and motioned Jill to go stand where I was, a little ways off, which she did. The truck came alongside, and came to a stop and the guy in the back stood up and leveled a deer rifle at us.

"Mornin'" he said, and that was all.

Two other guys, who don't deserve description, got out of the cab. One had another rifle and the other had a handgun.

I am now not remembering where I am. I am somewhere in a different timeline that is a threat to me and those I love. I am not here right now. I do nothing but stand.

"No time to chat. Buster, get their keys and wallets and anything else," said the man with the rifle who'd been driving.

Buster, I suppose, who was carrying the handgun, came around and collected what he wanted from our trucks and put them in the back of theirs. Then he came by and got my wallet and keys, which I handed to him without a word or a thought. He went on to Anders after me and Jill, and said "Stand up and give me your wallet."

Anders said "Can't. Hurt my leg. That's why I'm sitting dumbass."

He reached around and made a struggle of getting his wallet out, wincing as if in pain while he did so.

That's when a branch I'm almost one-hundred percent sure was broken on purpose made a loud crack down the road, and then there was Stacy, removing herself from the enclosing woods, standing in the road, twenty paces off with a double-barreled shotgun leveled at the guy who was giving the orders.

"Stand down," was all she said. Nothing else.

In that brief moment of distraction, Anders stood and grabbed Buster's wrist with his right hand, took his gun away, and with his left arm put a stranglehold on him and sat him in his lap as he sat back down on the tailgate. The guy was making gurgling sounds and it was clear Anders wasn't going to merely let him go, but probably strangle him to death with one arm.

In the confusion, Stacy had magically stepped ten paces closer. Anders trained his gun on the other rifleman who was now wanting to circle.

"Move again!" Anders shouted, "and I kill you!"

The fellow glanced at the other guy, the guy giving orders, and stood still.

Past present future. I don't know. I bent down and quickly picked up a rock, a good one, just the size of my hand, something big enough to throw, and I glanced quickly at Anders who just happened to be looking at me. Before I took my eyes away I thought I'd seen, just briefly, a nod from him. He had a tight grip around the man's neck who was sitting on his lap, and the revolver was easy in his other hand. I remember.

It was now, the present tense, I could feel it, see it for just a moment, certain of it. It seeped into me from somewhere and I just knew it.

"One more step girlie and a bullet in your gut," the order-giver guy said, looking at Stacy, his rifle leveled where he'd said.

"Shoot that other bastard!" he yelled over his shoulder, eyes foolishly away from Stacy, "Or the other two!"

Stacy made two more quick steps, shotgun leveled at his face, fifteen paces away.

"Cut you in half," she said with a voice like one of our dogs, angry.

The other guy, who was watching the three of us, kept moving his attention back and forth between

Stacy, Anders, and Jill and I. I looked over at Anders, who still had a death grip on the guy in his lap, and of the two riflemen, one stayed focused on Stacy and the other on Anders.

"Standoff girlie," the guy said facing Stacy. "Two and two. Get outta here and we'll be on our way."

And Anders, whose face was now something I never want to see again, glanced quickly at Stacy to catch her eye, and then raised his right arm, leveled, and fired at the other rifleman and blew out his hip. Stacy quickly moved ten paces closer while the other man with the rifle was distracted by the screaming of his buddy.

I need to pause here and say that being shot with a bullet is not at all what you see on television, where the hero has a bandage on his shoulder in the final scene and is fine after that. No, any shot from a high-powered weapon will either kill you from blood loss or later sepsis in the hospital or if you survive, leave you crippled for life begging for pain meds.

Anders, as cool and level as he was with a firearm, in my estimation could have just as easily murdered the other guy, but instead chose to put him in a wheelchair for the remainder of his life, and I think he may have known that. Perhaps it was only mercy, but he had such anger on his face, I don't know. I think he knew and made the choice he wanted.

And now, by the time he had his senses back again, Stacy's shotgun was in the other man's gut and she said "Call it."

The other man stood there, no longer a threat, but still held his weapon. A rock hit him in the back, just right on the spine, and he went down.

Anders stood and all in one motion pushed the man on his lap away from him and put the gun in his left hand and round-housed the guy with his right, and the fellow collapsed, yes, just kind of like you might see on television in this case.

Then, I don't know. There is some distance here for me where I am trying to recall where I am. I am hearing something. It's is shouting but it is coming from a great distance and I can't understand what it's saying. It's coming through the woods that may surround me, and it is not the voice of the river, the ceaseless and endless and ever-so-restful river. It is something else. I try to remember.

"Al! Al!" Stacy is shouting and is staring at me I don't know why, but there is a weight somewhere, a useless weight that I don't recognize right away, and I looked at Stacy and Jill and even Anders and they all had some sort of look on their faces that I couldn't understand.

I looked down and saw that I was straddling the man Anders had knocked out, standing just over his head, and I had a very heavy rock clasped between both hands, so heavy I could barely hold it.

I don't remember any more than that.

CHAPTER TWENTY:
HIDE AND SEEK

There's this one thing about life that remains a constant: nothing ever seems to go just the way you'd like it to. Oh, I know, you're going to say I'm being pessimistic and that on most days the truck does in fact start up and on most days the coffee pot works just fine and then there are all those times when you didn't get killed by a ricochet when Delmer was shooting gophers in his backyard and that I should be grateful instead. I know, I know. It's just that this whole thing with Kenna and Hollis makes me feel bad and I feel responsible for getting them together in the first place and now it seems like it's all gone south on them and they just got married and everything and somehow this is my fault along with hay bales, but there's nothing I can do about that. Or this either.

Like an idiot I'd told Kenna that I'd find Hollis somehow, and I didn't know how to do that. Like I was going to what? Run around in the woods looking for an ex-Army Ranger who obviously didn't want to be found?

Of course, the other constant in life is that things never go as expected, and that can be bad or good.

Among the unexpected is the fact that some little while after I had talked to Kenna I was sitting on The

Bench outside Del's with my sacred cup of morning coffee when who should be walking up the sidewalk but Stacy! To me, this was a miracle nearly as astounding as Moses speaking to a burning bush, because a regular person never sees Stacy, ever, unless she wants to be seen, and then to find her just walking down a sidewalk instead of on some mountaintop or in an old-growth forest in the wilderness was just beyond imagining.

She stopped when she got to The Bench and said

"Morning Al. How's Grip these days?"

I said he was just fine, but also that it seemed a little unusual for her to be here in town of all things.

"Just popped into the Safeway for supplies. Game Wardens eat too, you know. Thought I'd try the number six for breakfast."

"Hey, mind if I joined you for a few minutes?"

We went on in and Stacy sat at the bar instead of a booth, I guess she's used to being on her own, and so I did too.

Ricky swept by and took Stacy's order and I got some more coffee and Stacy said "So what is it? You look like you want to tell me something."

Now, I hadn't expected to actually meet Stacy like this of course, I mean, who would? So, I wasn't so sure how to ask if she could somehow be persuaded to help me find Hollis because she's out there in the mountains all the time and is a whole lot better tracker than those people you see in movies. But the problem was, the problem was, I had the feeling that Stacy kind of liked Hollis for some unfathomable reason, and then of course he and Kenna had gotten married, just like that, or so it might seem. Tact was important.

"I need to find Hollis. He's gone walkabout or whatever it is they say in Australian movies, and he told me that you'd ditch him every time when he was trying to find you. You're obviously a whole lot better than him at this hide-and-seek thing. I figure if there's anybody who can find an Army Ranger when he doesn't want to be found, it's you."

Stacy looked at her coffee and then drank it in a few swift swallows.

"It's not my business to find lost people Al, it's Walter's. He's the guy to talk to. I just look after the flora and the fauna and sometimes the flotsam, like yourself," and she smiled.

Okay, she had me there. But no way Walter had the kind of skills that I needed. Stacy did.

"Alright, I know what you're saying, but of course Walter isn't going to go looking for Hollis in the territory you cover. Can you just, you know, kind of keep an eye out for him or something and let me know?"

"Sure, Al. I can do that. Maybe meet me here every Tuesday and I'll catch you up on what I know."

Stacy's #6 arrived via Ricky with a flourish, and also had a Nasturtium flower sitting on the extra-crispy hash browns.

I looked up at Ricky and said "What the heck? I don't get edible flowers on my hash browns."

Ricky wasn't looking at me, and instead at Stacy.

"Stacy's only in once a week," Ricky said, "so she's special." And he walked away and didn't even refill my coffee.

Definitely something in the water in Dobbins these days.

I came into Del's the next Tuesday, and behold! Stacy was there! I eagerly went up and sat down a stool next to her.

"Hi Stacy, how you doing? Anything to report?"

Stacy crumpled a piece of bacon and had it in a single bite, and had another forkful of hash browns to boot.

"Sorry," she said while chewing. "Busy day. Gotta run soon and no, haven't seen a thing. Well, except these huge, almost man-like footprints in the mud next to Spotted Lake up in the high plateau. Just huge you know?" she said and swallowed. "Biggest darn footprints I've ever seen."

Stacy looked sideways at me, but I wasn't going for it.

"I'm recently from Oregon," I said. "Spent thirty-five years in the PNW."

"Dang!" Stacy said. "But no, sorry, nothing I can help you with. Haven't seen a thing."

Chuck took me on down to Del's the next Tuesday, and as always, he parked himself under a tree across the street instead of the parking lot. He just doesn't care for parking lots you see. I'm not sure what it is, but that's okay with me.

Sure enough, there was Stacy, and when she saw me she said "Al! Al, I have something to tell you! Let's get a booth okay?"

You have to realize that I was so excited to hear her say this, because it meant she had at least some sort of knowledge about where Hollis was, and then maybe, if he wasn't so very far out somewhere in the wilderness, then maybe I could somehow track him down and talk with him and get him to come home and start talking to Kenna again, because that's what she wanted, and I owed it to both of them, somehow. Some sort of reckoning anyway.

Well, we got ourselves a booth and Stacy was really excited, I mean just about to bust, and I had a big smile on my face in anticipation.

"So tell me, go ahead!"

Stacy took a swig of coffee and said, kind of all-a-fluster actually, which sort of surprised me, "So, you don't know my daily routines of course and so I'll say that I was over at Roundabout," and then she stopped herself and said "Ha! That's silly. That's just what I call the place, I mean it's actually, well, you know grid 5470 on your GPS and, now I realize you probably don't know about that either," she said seeing my smile evaporate for a bit, "but that's okay. I'm just trying to say that's where I met Clark."

Stacy smiled and looked at me, as if that explained everything somehow, which of course it didn't. Stacy smiled.

"Stacy, I have no idea what you're talking about."

"Oh!" she said, her reverie broken.

She proceeded to tell me about being out someplace in the wilderness and she was on a stake-out of sorts because some poaching had been going on in that area, and Stacy takes a very dim view of poaching to say the least. Anyway, she said she was in her Juniper Bush outfit, because it was one of her favorites ("No berries, of course. Wrong time of year."), and was walking through the woods to get to where she wanted to be when she heard someone say "Good morning! That's really great camo by the way!"

"Al, I just about jumped out of my skin at that, and I turned and looked everywhere, but I couldn't see anything. Nothing at all! It was amazing!"

And then she went on to tell me how a tree suddenly detached itself from the rest of the woods and strode over to her.

"It was like the Wizard of Oz or something!" she gushed.

And apparently the tree introduced itself and said he was a wildlife biologist and was on loan from Penn State and was studying the mating habits of Grizzlies, if that was even possible, and of course had spent some time on his camo, you know, because of mating Grizzlies of course. Certainly want to be on the down-low taking pictures of that.

"Well his outfit was just amazing Al! I'd never seen anything like that before. I mean, he really looked exactly like a tree and everything, and his name is Clark. I thought that was really something because you don't hear people called Clark very much anymore do you? I mean of course there's Clark Gable and Clark Kent and everything, so who would have thought! I want to introduce you! You should see his tree camo!"

"But Stacy, what about Hollis?"

"What? Who?"

"Hollis, you know, I asked if you'd keep an eye out for Hollis."

"Oh," Stacy said, "Haven't seen him."

CHAPTER TWENTY-ONE:
WHY MONTANA DRIVERS ARE THE FRIENDLIEST IN THE COUNTRY

When Joanie and I first arrived in Montana one of the things we noticed right away was that when you met an oncoming vehicle the driver invariably raised a hand as a wave as you passed by. This happens on 81, our local byway, but also on country and mountain roads, as well as stretches of interstate here and there. Once we found ourselves headed south from Butte to Idaho Falls on the interstate and even though the four lanes are separated by a considerable median, folks headed north would invariably wave at us, and sometimes even people who passed us would give a brief wave.

In my state of mind I always worried that maybe something was wrong with the car and people were trying to alert us to smoke coming from the back or something though I never made these fears known because Joanie always said "That's really something. People are so friendly out here. I think it's just great."

But it was later, I'm pretty sure it was later because I can't keep up with this whole past present future thing anymore like I used to, but once when I was driving along on 81 and someone raised their hand in our little Montana salute as she passed by I just wondered. I wondered if maybe we did that so we'd be seen. I wondered that if you weren't like, you know, really seen and acknowledged by someone else then maybe you didn't really exist. You know, you thought you were alive and all but you know that old conundrum about a tree falling in the woods. I just wondered about that is all.

I made sure I waved at everyone, all the time, without fail. Just in case. Of course, everyone knows Chuck. They just don't know me all that well.

It was that morning heading down into town, just a trip to the Safeway, when Chuck started to list just a bit and I pulled over and took a look around and sure enough his left front tire was about halfway down and going down quickly. I got the jack as quickly as I could and got it set because the flatter a tire gets the more you have to jack it up, and I'm a thoughtful and fore-sightful and lazy person at heart.

So, yes, I know you're amazed that I did this given my earlier explanations about my mechanical skills, but I'm not entirely helpless on most days, on most days anyway, and besides I keep the jack and the spare and that thing that looks a bit like Norse insignia of Thor's hammer with holes in it in the back of the truck. You know. I'm thinking about things, like in advance, like future tense is all I'm saying.

So, I've got the jack in place and was just about to get Thor's hammer because there are things you're supposed to do with it, and I mostly know what these are but given my aptitude perhaps sacrifices will need to be made and some certain old words chanted, and that's when Walter pulled up behind me. He got out and walked up.

"Need any help, Al?"

I looked at him for a moment, struggling with the first lug-nut and said, "Oh, maybe. Maybe some moral support. I don't have any, you know?"

And I thought I'd done my best sarcastic grin but Walter just looked at me, and maybe through me, because he didn't seem so very, well, engaged, if you know what I mean. In fact, if I hadn't stood up right then and said yes, that would be great, could you help me, I think he'd have quickly turned around, gotten back in his truck, and I guess headed off to the rest of his very busy morning in Dobbins.

And so he did, because I am so very much older than him, and I'll tell you right now that when you have the option of doing something yourself or having someone thirty years younger do it for you you're an absolute fool for not going for option two. That way, later on in bed, you don't have to wonder "Why do I hurt so much? I only..." whatever it was. Anyway.

So there's Walter, and he's changing my tire, and I can tell you right now that he is very happy to do so, in fact far happier than any possible Good Samaritan you might ever run into except the mass killer sort should be, and this just disturbs the heck out of me.

I don't know what it is because I can't think too far about other people these days, maybe it was one of those blasted meteorites again or something, but I say:

"Walter. Have you ever gone on vacation? You know, just you and Veronica off at Yellowstone or wherever?

Maybe take a plane trip somewhere and get out and see what's there? That kind of thing?"

Walter never stopped turning the tire-iron. Not for a moment.

He gave a snort.

"Huh! Like who's going to replace me right? What's gonna happen if I'm not here?"

Well, I had to wonder about that somewhat, but even so I got down on my knees just like he was and said "Listen. Dobbins will be fine without you for just fourteen days. Just fourteen days. We'll be fine. Trust me. Call somebody! Tell them that you have to have your scheduled time off or something. Don't you think Veronica would like that? Wouldn't she like to get away and do something interesting? Wouldn't you, you know, just for a bit? Go sight-seeing or fishing or paddle a canoe on a quiet lake or something?"

Walter did not look at me and cinched the last lug nut and then let down the jack. He put the jack and tire iron and the tire in Chuck's bed without looking at me and then he went and got into his truck and drove off. He never said another word.

I think I've told you already, or maybe I will at some later point, I can't figure that stuff out any more, but I'm pretty sure I've already said that I don't know what's going on and how I can tell you about what happened when Walter called it a day and headed home. Whatever is going on, I can say a bit of something about that.

Walter pulled into the driveway as he has done had done will do just as he always has, had and will, and just almost the same time, except when he couldn't, and Veronica knew all that and knew that she shouldn't expect him to be just right-on-time-Walter, you know, because of his job and everything. And Veronica knew this of course, and she knew Walter was out and on most days was doing Good Things and Fighting the Good Fight that they both believed in, and so that was how it had to go. And she also knew that she was deeply in love with both Walter and the triplets and that she was worn down to the bone. She knew Walter couldn't be there like he said he wanted to be, but that didn't help very much.

It didn't help at all, in fact, and she spent most of her day running in six different directions and discovered there were whole new vistas of mathematic probability that she hadn't studied in college and of the ones she had studied none of them had anything to do with preparing you for triplets.

Tell the truth, Veronica was pretty much done-in every day when Walter came home, but he didn't seem to notice somehow. Oh sure, he laughed and played with the kids and was a great Dad and all, and he'd ask about her day and she might just have enough energy left to tell him a thing or two and he always said the right things in response to that and hugged her and told her how wonderful she was and Veronica wondered just why in the hell he didn't seem to get it and what the hell was wrong with him. But Walter was just Walter, she said, and such a wonderful guy and father. And the days and weeks and months and seasons went by.

And Walter pulled into the driveway. Did. Always had. Will do so again, just when he can or would or should. And I don't know what really happened, but maybe it was the mirror just inside the doorway to their house where Walter hung up his hat and holster every night and then walked into the house, and then on this night, whenever that was, he looked up and saw himself and saw that he hadn't seen, at least not for a while anyway.

And then Veronica appeared in the hallway, his beautiful Veronica, and maybe, I don't know, but maybe he just loved her so much that he never saw, I mean he never really saw, because his eyes only saw beautiful Veronica and could never see anything else. But something shifted, maybe because he'd just seen himself, and he saw how tired she was, so very tired, and her sweatshirt was stained with a day's worth of triplets, and Walter finally saw.

He put his hat away, the hat that meant who he was beyond that doorway of theirs, and he came to Veronica and said nothing at first but merely stroked her hair and then he hugged her.

"I have an idea," he said. "Let's go away for a couple of weeks. Just you and me. We can figure it out, I'm sure. Wouldn't that be nice?"

Veronica stepped back out from his embrace and looked him in the eye with disbelief, which melted to something else.

"Really? That would be wonderful."

CHAPTER TWENTY-TWO:
THE ASPEN GROVE

There is a place I know that no one knows. It is, because everything is. I got there first by not trying to. It is the aspen grove. You can't go there. It's one of those places near to where I hike miles into to get to the river. It is on someone's ranch I suppose because everything is. You can't get there if you try to. You can only get there when you aren't paying attention. I end up there when I have to.

The first time I got there was in the half-light of a new day, when the world rested in shadow and my boots were covered in dew. It was budding summer then if I recall correctly, though it wasn't very long ago, and I walked my walk to where I wanted to be. The river was in front of me some ways ahead.

But where you want to be isn't the same as where you should be, and some of you are old enough to know what I'm talking about, and so all I want to say is that I sort of wasn't looking very hard at where I was supposed to go and I guess I made a right when I should have gone left. I was on my well-worn path and then I wasn't.

This track I walk is the same one I've walked many times before. I can do it in the dark, and have. That's why I was surprised, when the light got a little better, that I wasn't where I wanted to be, but somewhere else.

I came to a jack-fence of logs, sagging in place, keeping in nothing any longer and keeping nothing out that wanted in. Beyond it was a meadow and aspen grove. It was an aspen grove that didn't belong here. This was the wrong ground, wrong altitude and wrong everything. It shouldn't be here. But it was, and it ached with tall grass and new leaves, and a tiny breeze, the first breath of dawn, swept through the leaves and they sang. I forgot about the river.

I stood there looking at it and then propped my rod against the poor old fence and climbed through the logs, hoping that they wouldn't give way to my touch. They were old, and whatever place this once was, was no longer here. Only the aspens. I stood on the other side. I walked in a little ways, and found a stump. I sat down in the new day, with nothing but the sound of leaves parleying to one another, all around me.

Here was only the Great Green Song, which is different from the sort that I only hear when I'm at The River, because that song is about forever and forever, and I can't listen for too very long. Here, the song was of now. It was different. It was not Then–Now–Tomorrow. Only Now. The white-white of the aspen bark was only green in this light, this first light. All of the light was green, nothing but. The sun had no power here to assert itself into another sort of light. No, it was only the Great Green.

I was sitting on a stump, in a ring of trees, and there was nothing else, no birdsong in this light, it was just the leaves in the breeze. They sang the song of the new earth, awakening, quickening, alive so that all else could live again. The song bore down into the ground and the stones and the grass itself sang, I could see it! Dancing in the new light of day. It thrummed in me. I felt it like my own heart. I closed my eyes, sleepy suddenly, carried along by the song.

I think I may have nodded off there for a bit. I was vaguely aware that perhaps I was trespassing on someone's place where I shouldn't be, but I couldn't make myself get up and leave. I'd gone the wrong way, certainly, and could be forgiven for that, if nothing else. I sat on the stump.

I keep wanting to tell you things but I don't know how. I keep wanting to not tell myself things and I'm good at it. I only wish I could just say, whenever this was, what happened.

No, there were no Druids who woke the Green with their ash-wands that day. There were no fairy folk or lights or even the sense of being swept away in a river, The River, wherever it now was in my reckoning. No, none of that. That was all before and after. It was only a bit of nodding off, a bit of peace, a little something that I want to stop talking about because I just can't. I've lied to you so many times and right now, just right now, I won't lie about the aspen grove.

The breeze died. I felt sleepy. I roused myself and I stood beyond all reckoning and got myself out of there, and back on the way that I wanted instead of where I didn't want and got back on my way. But I came there again, not when I wanted, but when I should. That's the way it goes. You can never know.

CHAPTER TWENTY-THREE:
STANDING IN THE LIGHT

Socrates once said that the unexamined life is not worth living. I'm not real sure about that, but I do know it can get you in trouble if you don't. When I look back on the not-so-distant-me, it seems as if my recent track record has been a track record: I run away. I get scared about things and I run away from them. I get angry and try to run away from that too. I get worn out having to face things and I run away. I get confused or just stupid and running is all there is. I'm getting good at it I suppose. I've worn out a couple of pairs of shoes doing it. The problem with running away from things isn't always what it is you're running from, but rather the fact that you don't know where it is that you're running to. You thought you were just side-stepping the Poison Oak on the trail, but because you weren't looking, I mean really looking, that's when you went over the cliff.

Even so, when you're looking, and you know what you're seeing, sometimes you still just can't see or believe it.

Things were getting so bad between me and Joanie that when I suggested that I might want to camp a couple of days and do some extended fishing before the summer got too far along she helped me pack. Before I knew it she had most of the camping gear stowed in Chuck's bed so that there wasn't much left for me to do except get my fishing gear and put some food in a cooler.

I mentioned that I wasn't necessarily planning on leaving right *then,* but Joanie said "Summer's getting along. Better get out there while you've got the chance, right?"

There really wasn't any argument about this, and I guess I wanted to get away for a while just as much as she wanted me to, so I got the rest of my stuff and said my goodbyes and headed down to the Safeway for supplies.

When I'm off by myself I pretty much eat "guy food"; you know, the sort of things that just don't require much skill or thought to cook. I mean, the whole point of being out camping and doing whatever it is that you went there for, is not about seeing if you can make something fancy over hot coals. Ideally, you'd like something that goes in a single pot or a frying pan, and because that's all I brought with me that's exactly what I did: meat, potatoes, rudimentary breakfast items, and sandwich stuff for lunch: you can always stick a sandwich in your fly vest somewhere if the fishing's good. Chuck and I pulled into the Safeway and I got my supplies and headed back to the parking lot.

So, after that I just pointed Chuck in the direction of the wilderness, which is pretty much any direction depending on how far you want to go, and we headed out of town. I knew a nice little mountain lake way up in the Rockies with just one or two campsites and suggested that to Chuck, and you could fly fish the lake if you wanted but for me there were several small rivers in the area, and creeks that I knew ran in and out of the lake that I wanted to try out.

It was late afternoon when Chuck and I finally zigged and zagged our way up a rocky forest service road and found the two campsites, both unoccupied. Chuck pulled us up close to the lake and then I started getting the tent set up.

The whole point of going camping is of course "getting away from it all," which typically means something along the lines of leaving your cares behind and relaxing in a frustration-free environment. Putting up a tent by yourself challenges this whole idea. I laid the tent out and then started putting the poles together to slide through those little sleeves for them and then had to try to stick them in little pockets on each corner. You know the poles I'm talking about, right? The real bendy ones that are strung together with little bungy cords for whatever insane reason they are. At first I thought that was just so they'd kind of stay together, you know? So that you didn't lose some critical part of your tent. But no, that's not it. You could have put just plain old string inside them for that. The reason they're strung together with elastic lines is because it's a test. The folks who make these things want to see just exactly who they're dealing with, and maybe they've also had some experiences with "the bad camping neighbor" and they'd sort of like to cull the herd a bit. That's what I'm thinking. That's also why they make the poles just a little bit too long to fit in the pockets once you have them put together.

Anyway, I'd get one of the poles put together and then carefully slide it into its pocket on the far end and then bow it up with all my might and with quavering arms try to get the blasted thing into the pocket just a mere two inches away and then shout some choice imprecations as the whole blasted tent slid sideways.

This happened several times and then I looked up and saw Chuck was just standing there, kind of looking sideways at me with something that appeared to be the birth of a grin on his front end and I looked back at him and said it wasn't funny and if he thought it was he should give it a go himself. So, Chuck decided to finally help and he braced the far end of a pole against his tire and then the tent wouldn't go sliding away and I pushed and pushed and the pole was bending pretty good now and I could just about get it in the little pocket just an inch away, and do you have any idea how fast those little spring-loaded poles can go if you lose your grip? Go right through you if you were standing just-so. Chuck thought it was extremely funny, but only because he doesn't need a tent. I said something about locking the garage door and he mumbled something about something and then we did it again.

Once the tent was finally up and I put my cot inside with the sleeping bag (yes, there's a cot, I'm not one of those like real wilderness people you read about in a book by Hemingway or Crane) then it was finally time to you know, get away from it all. I pulled out a folding chair and sat down, looking out at the most beautiful little mountain lake you might imagine, just almost a bowl of bright blue water scooped out of a half-ring of rocky peaks. It was not the time of day to fish, and it was too early to think about cooking something, and so I just sat there in the pines in the warm air with the blue, blue lake glistening in the late afternoon sun, just right in front of me, and it was all so terribly boring.

Normally at this point Joanie and I would be taking the dogs for a walk in the woods and exploring our environs, and so since I was without both Joanie and the dogs, I figured I'd better get up and start exploring my environs. That's what one does when they're camping after all. I mean, you can't just sort of sit there staring at a lake for very long now can you?

I walked around the campsite first and saw pine needles and bits of bark and some mushrooms of the sort that would kill you if you even looked at them too long. Then I walked a bit of a trail in the woods that ran along the lake. I spotted quite a lot of pine needles and bark there. I also saw some flowers and thought I'd better go back and get my camera to take a picture of them. I did that and I think I chewed up, oh, maybe twenty-five minutes or so. I sat in my chair and stared at the lake.

Eventually I figured that maybe I'd better do this whole "extended fishing" trip that I presumably came out here for, and so I got my rod and got into my gear and headed off to where I knew a nice river entered the lake. It wasn't easy getting there and I had to do quite a bit of bushwhacking to do so, but hey, I had nothing but time on my hands.

I did in fact catch some nice fish once I got to the river, and I kept four of them. I almost never keep any fish except on rare occasions, and I had in mind that this might be one of them. I took them back to my campsite, cleaned them and put them on ice, sat back in my chair and opened a beer and stared at the lake for a while longer.

About an hour later I gathered up what I thought was probably enough firewood to last twenty people a long night's carouse next to a fire, and then, as the sun was just about headed over the ridge, I got the fire going and fired up a lantern. I cut up some potatoes and put them in a pan, I wrapped the trout in foil with some herbs and butter, and then I sat back down. I had just opened another beer when I heard some heavy foot-steps in the woods nearby.

"You're not doing much of a job sneaking up on someone for an Army Ranger," I said.

"Only because I was hoping I wouldn't have to kill you just to get something to eat," Hollis said as he emerged from the woods and into the firelight.

"There's a beer in the cooler," I said, not getting up.

Hollis walked over, got one, and sat down on the folding chair that I had brought for him, on the oppo-site side of the fire.

"Thanks," he said. And that was it and now I supposed it was all up to me.

Hollis had quite a bit of beard now as you might ex-pect, and yet he didn't look like someone from ZZ Top so I assumed he'd been taking care of himself as best he could, at least on occasion.

I didn't know much what to say, I hardly ever do any-more it seems like, so all I could ask was "How's it been going?"

"Just great," he said. "Yep, just great."

We looked at one another for a while, neither one of

us knowing what to say for some stupid reason, but Hollis saved the day by saying "I'm hungry. You gonna cook something? Maybe talk after that?"

That seemed like a good idea to me and so I set my beer down on the Forest Service picnic table, which isn't really so much a "table" as it is a slab of wood, six inches thick, bolted together with titanium, and which is a testament to both the fact that the Forest Service doesn't make junk, they never do, and also the idea that there's no way they're putting up with any idle vandalism. No, if the Forest Service had been in charge of it all, we'd still be on the Moon. With really nice picnic tables.

I looked up then and noticed for the first time that my little campsite was completely ringed with boulders. My own little henge. Those Forest Service folks think of everything.

I stirred the coals, put on the potatoes and set the foil-wrapped trout a bit to the side and then sat back down and stared at them. What else was there to do? From time to time I stirred the potatoes.

"I came because I saw you here before, at least around here, maybe over the next ridge, and I wanted to talk to you. I told Kenna I'd find you and bring you home because she wants to talk to you."

Hollis didn't say anything for a while, just looked at his hands, feet, maybe the nearest tree or the ring of rocks. "How're the potatoes looking?"

Eventually we ate and it looked as though Hollis might have been missing meals because he had three fish to my one, and most of the potatoes. I thought he might also chug the ketchup as desert.

We put the plates up, sat back down on either side of the fire, and then I said again: "I told Kenna I'd find you. I said I'd get you back home. She says she just wants to talk. She's worried about you."

Hollis scowled and said "Huh. That doesn't sound right. Last thing I remember was bein' told to get out and never come back."

"I know. I talked to her. She was still pretty worked up even then," and I went on to tell him about what I'd seen at the Curl Up and Dye between her and Dreama. Hollis actually looked a bit worried about that, I don't know. He's hard to read.

"Anyway, she was crying and I said I'd find you, and now I have."

Hollis pushed his hat back, "Kenna say what was going on? What was wrong? Because that's what I can't figure out and I thought it was best for me to just get out like she said and maybe at least give her some peace or something."

I told him then a bit about what I'd overheard at her shop, and a bit about what she'd told me that day. Hollis shook his head.

"Got any more beer?" he asked.

"No," I said, but got up and got my duffle bag from Chuck and sat back down with it.

I really have no idea why, but for some reason I'd been hauling around in my camping duffle for the longest time a bottle of something that Joanie and I never, ever drink. I don't know. Maybe I thought that if we were in dire need I could start a fire with it or something, or maybe douse an open wound like they do in the old westerns. It was a bottle of something along the lines of Old Gramaw's Velvet Elixir, or something like that.

Anyway, there was probably a little skull and crossbones on it somewhere, but it was dark and so I couldn't read the appropriate warning label. I handed it over to Hollis. He held it up to the light for a moment and then unscrewed the top. And why is it that a nice bottle of wine takes a corkscrew and some actual effort to open, while something that might kill you opens with the flick of the wrist? I'm just asking is all.

Hollis said "I never drink this stuff. Not since Afghanistan or something anyway. Probably a good idea."

He had a drink and then reached across the fire with it to me, carefully so that it didn't combust in our faces, and I did too. That went on for some little while until Hollis leaned forward in his chair and said "Okay," and he started talking. We passed the bottle back and forth between us most of the time.

What he told me was that after the wedding everything was good, better than good, and he was so happy and so was Kenna he thought, and then as the winter months went by he thought she was kind of unhappy, or maybe just less so, but he didn't know why. He said Kenna had come to him at some point and asked him why he wasn't happy and why he didn't talk to her as much and he said that of course he was and of course he did and he shook his head and said he didn't understand what she was talking about.

And he went on, and I handed him the bottle again, and he said well you know what I'm talking about right? You told me and I can't explain to anybody what happened in those years and how it tears you up inside, and so sure, sometimes I'd go off by myself or something because that's probably the best thing to do, right? And he handed me the bottle and I said sure, I know what you mean, and he said there's nothing wrong with it you just have to deal with it and it's not like anyone can see it anyway, and so you just man-up, right?

I said my own strategy was running and he looked at me a bit and then started laughing. That's right, he said, I forgot, and then I said something else I don't remember what but Hollis went quiet then. Then he said that he honestly thought that maybe he'd better get out of Kenna's way for a while and that he thought that would be good for him too, you know, just have a little quiet time or something like that.

Hollis shook his head as he handed me the bottle and said "Because I sure don't want to upset her. I don't. She's changed me and helped me and I don't want anything that would hurt her. It's just that I am and I don't know why! I can't see it or understand it or somethin.'"

He sat back down and rubbed his face and then put his hands through his hair and stared at the fire.

He looked at the ground, his hands, a tree, the darkness maybe inside, and said "So how do you do it? You and Joanie have been married since the 80's you said. How do you do it? I don't know what to do."

And then I told him that I had essentially kicked myself out of the house, and if you can believe it, Hollis' mouth hung open for a minute. He closed his mouth and handed me the bottle.

"I don't believe it," he said. "I thought you two were, you know, happily ever after and all that."

And so I told him. I told him about my school and my friend and the day the killer came and what I saw as best as I could remember. I told him how I couldn't think or feel anymore like I used to. I told him how I couldn't make Joanie happy anymore because I'd forgotten how to or forgotten how to care or forgotten that there was anybody left alive but me. I told him about fishing and why I go as often as I can. I told him about how I don't want to think about things very much if I don't have to and that I don't even like watching the news if I can help it. I told him that I didn't listen to Linda, my therapist, because I couldn't listen or think and that I had lied to Joanie and said that it was my therapist's advice that we move here, just because I thought I needed to run away and start all over. And I told him that he was right about what he'd told me before, about how you can't run away from trauma and how it just follows you around. And I told him that I knew I was losing Joanie because I hadn't been there for her these past two years, not the way she had been there for me, and that I didn't know what to do to make things right again. I told him I didn't know where I am was will be anymore.

Hollis had been silent the entire time, but then he sat back a bit, just a bit, thinking I suppose.

He said, "I know what you mean about the news. Nothin' good there."

Then he sagged a bit, looked up: "But there's no way I'm going to hug you or something like that if that's what you're thinking. I've been in plenty of hospitals where we're all wounded and after a while nobody tries to compare wounds. What the hell's the point anyway? I mean, you know better than anybody where you hurt. Why try to explain it to somebody else?"

Hollis leaned forward on his chair then, looking down at his hands I suppose, and then the rest of what happened you're going to have to write off as alcohol or something, except that we were both there and we knew what we saw, and later we talked about it, but just between ourselves.

The campfire had gotten down to just that perfect red glow that one might imagine in a painting, with just enough blue red yellow flame to give off a light that showed the two of us to each other in the same colors, and a few sparks leapt off a crackling piece of wood as it settled deeper into the fire pit.

That's when the little lights, maybe a dozen of them, pink and blue and yellow, began to descend from the trees and hang in the air between us. Just hanging there. And then they began to move, as if in some sort of swirling dance that perhaps if you could see it from up above made some kind of pattern just beyond the reckoning of what you might imagine.

The little lights descended, and they danced and swirled and we were mesmerized. At last a little pink maybe blue light twinkled onto Hollis' shoulder and just sat there. Hollis raised his hand to sweep it away.

I said "Don't," for whatever reason there might have been.

Hollis sat dead-still, his eyes on nothing at all, and then he said "It's talking to me. It's saying something."

I watched. Hollis' mouth moved without saying anything. The other lights danced and moved about the fire, sometimes darting here and there, but the one on

Hollis' shoulder stayed. Eventually, it lifted from his shoulder, slowly made a circuit of his head, and then sped away into the trees. As if that was a signal, then all the other little lights rose up from wherever they were, swirled around my head one last moment, and chased away in pursuit. No lights, I thought later, had settled on me.

Hollis stood then, a look of utter bewilderment on his face at first and then that resolved into something else.

"I've been such an ass" he said. "I have to go. Now. Right now."

I stood then too and said "But Hollis, now? It's the middle of the night! Get some sleep and then tomor-row..."

"No, now. Thanks Al." There was something in his eyes. Maybe it was absolutely nothing, and that scared me a bit.

And then he walked into the woods, and then I heard him splashing through the river that let out from the lake, and then I heard nothing. I stood for a bit, and turned my back to the fire. There in front of me my shadow played out elongated on the ground, but nothing so much as my long, long ears, which stood out up above my head for anyone who could to see.

CHAPTER TWENTY-FOUR:
CHIP COMES AROUND

One day somewhere still during winter, which could of course have been anywhere from October to May, and I just don't remember is all, I went down to The Paper to turn in my column on a Wednesday before the Friday-night print and Saturday distribution. I was pretty excited about this column because I had heard about a fellow, almost over in Butte he was so far away, who people said could bend a horseshoe in his bare hands before you could say "What the hell?"

So, I made the long, long drive over to his place, and turns out this guy's a plumber when he apparently isn't amazing folks with his manual prowess. So, I pulled up in his driveway, and Chuck parked and I got out and started walking to his front door, but I saw he had his garage door open and was there already waiting for me.

I walked on up and introduced myself, and he did the same and we shook hands and he didn't seem to grip my hand in some sort of death-grip which I've kind of gotten used to since we moved out here. And of course, I was sort of expecting him to show me right off how powerful he was, but he didn't do that. Instead he just walked over to his work bench, picked up a horseshoe, and handed it to me. Yep, it was a normal horseshoe. I handed it back and if I hadn't seen it myself I wouldn't have believed it, because all he did was grip both horns in each hand and twist, and it happened as fast as you or I might crumple a piece of tin foil. He almost both completely flattened the horseshoe as well as turned it into a screw. I was amazed.

We talked for quite a bit about this for my column you know, and he said that actually it wasn't all that many years ago that he even discovered he could do this. He'd been on a plumbing job and had just discovered that he had mis-cut a piece of iron pipe and that it was now completely useless and he said he just got mad and before he knew what had happened he'd pretty much turned the pipe into a metal bow-tie. I believed him too.

And what was really interesting was that this guy was no strong-man either. I mean, he was no huge, powerful person like Einar or Hollis, and he could no more have picked up a tree stump and lugged it a few feet than anyone else. He was just an average-looking guy. So I asked him about that, about how he could somehow twist a horseshoe with his bare hands before you could even blink. He said he didn't really know, and that maybe it was because he didn't think he couldn't, and that maybe he simply believed he could. I started to wonder if there was anything to that whole mind-over-matter business after all.

When I came in the office door I only saw Jeff at his desk, which was kind of unusual.

"Chip out sick today?" I said.

Jeff frowned a bit at that.

"You could say so. Love-sick anyway. He's in back hanging out. Meanwhile, I'm writing a newspaper."

"Oh," I said, sitting down. "So he's still pretty unhappy with Jill sort of dating that Anders guy, huh?"

"He definitely hit the moping stage anyway. I guess he's tried calling her once or twice but she hasn't been returning his calls, and whenever he sort of casually strolls into the Safeway hoping to just coincidentally meet she's not there. And as near as I can tell Jill isn't 'sort of' dating him. I saw them a few days ago and they looked pretty close if you know what I mean."

"Hmmm," I said. "Maybe I'll just go on back and see how he's doing."

I wandered through the back door into the warehouse part of the building, past piles and piles of refuse, and also some of Chip and Jeff's piles of prior ways to kill themselves while still enjoying some sort of demented competition they'd had going since childhood. That's a bit of a story itself, and doesn't figure in here I'm afraid. But as I made my way back through the rundown, concrete block building, the light only making a brief foray through the tiny and stained rectangular windows up above, I saw a light a little further on and made my way there, and there was Chip, looking at the wreckage of his sled from the Mc-Masters run a little over a year ago. He'd healed up just nicely from that, by the way.

"Hi Chip," I said as I arrived. "How's it going?" and I found a pile of something to sit on nearby, maybe what was left of Jeff's sled.

"Oh, hi Al," he said without looking up. "Didn't hear you come in."

I'm going to have to stop and digress for a bit here before we go on, and even though I want to tell you about Chip and what happened, what I saw in Chip made me both want to commiserate with him and also just get up and walk the other way. And you don't have to tell me how disappointed you are in me for feeling the need to just leave him on his own, sort of wounded soldier on the battlefield or something like that. It's just that I don't look in the mirror anymore, whatever timeline this is, because if I do, if I do, then I am quite literally and metaphorically facing myself and I'm still way too messed up to do that. And looking at Chip, this nice guy, this really fun guy, and how miserable he was, he was just a mirror and it was hard to face.

"I see you're looking at the wreckage of the past," I said, "and you don't need to be a genius to figure out the symbolism there, right?"

Chip just nodded a bit, but ran a hand down his broken sled, a chance for glory or something, perhaps only equaling himself in his mind to Jeff again, his best friend since childhood, and then of course Jill. I don't actually know what he may have felt for her or how he imagined things might go, I suppose none of us can, but he was hurting and I did not in fact stand and rest a hand on his shoulder as I'm assuming you think I might have. No. That does no good. Trust me.

Instead, I simply stood up and walked back down the debris-strewn aisle in the dark, back to the office where Jeff was sitting at his desk, typing away. I came in and pulled a chair up to Jeff's desk, and did so with as many scrapes and screeches that I could manage on the wooden floor. Jeff of course, as desired, looked up at me with a puzzled face.

I looked at him and said, for whatever reasons that were now percolating in me, and I really can't say where they came from, not all anyway, "This is all your fault you know."

You see? I was too weak to carry anyone else, but Jeff was strong, and besides, it was his to carry, and I hope both you and he can forgive me, at least some day.

Jeff as you might imagine just sat straight in his chair with a look of utter surprise on his face.

"What? What are you talking about? He's sad. He'll get over it. We have a newspaper to get out! He needs to just get over it and get going again!" he said with some emphasis.

I sat there and looked at Jeff, just right in the eyes because I knew I had to, and then down at the floor.

"Sorry Jeff," I said. "I just thought you'd be looking out for him. You know, find a way to distract him a bit so that he doesn't end up just wallowing in his unhappiness. Sorry. That's all."

I stood and turned to go and Jeff stood up and said "Well I've been trying to! He just doesn't want to play ice-frisbee and stuff anymore!"

"You'll find something," I said. "Oh yes, I know you will." I walked out the door.

It was maybe three weeks later when I got the call from Jeff about coming up over by ours and Delmer's place where there weren't any barbed-wire fences and I reassured him there weren't, and that it was all "open ground" up here, you know, no one's ranch or anything like that, and as far as I knew, no fences between here and Dobbins.

"Nothing kind of prickly up there at all?" Jeff asked.

"No, not that I'm aware of, "

Jeff said "That's perfect."

And that was all.

Next day, Chip and Jeff arrived in their tiny little car, which in my opinion was something that no one in their right mind would attempt to drive in Montana, and yet they did, and apparently went wherever they needed to go at whatever season and in whatever need.

They pulled up in my driveway as planned, and then Chuck and I followed them down a bit of a hill from our place, and then went west a bit and then pulled off in a pasture I wasn't familiar with. Jeff got out first and then so did I and finally Chip, and Jeff said "Can you help me get these out a bit?"

I didn't know what this was but we somehow extracted from their itty-bitty car two large wads of folded plastic, and then Jeff plugged a tiny little compressor into the cigarette lighter, or whatever was the equivalent these days, and started to inflate one, very slowly.

"So what's this?" I said, and Jeff, just all nonchalant, even though we standing up here in winter and freezing, said "Just some inflatable balls. You'll see."

So, Jeff got these huge plastic balls blown up in maybe twenty-five minutes or so, and kept reassuring both Chip and me that it would be worth the wait. While we were waiting, I surveyed the landscape of the pasture and noted that there was a small pond not far away which not-so-inexplicably was ice-free, given that there were cows all over the place here. I noticed that the ground gave away a bit further out, giving a bit of a slope. I had no idea what lay beyond that.

Finally, Jeff had two gigantic balls, maybe seven feet high, filled with air. They were chambered in some way like a giant spherical bubble-pack of some sort.

"Now what," said Chip, hands in his pockets, hunched in the cold.

"Watch," Jeff said, and he opened a flap on one side of a ball and got inside and stood in the middle of the ball and closed the flap. He was surrounded on all sides by the giant bubbles that made up the ball.

"Look!" he said and just started walking and he just rolled along!

Chip laughed and shouted at him, "That's awesome!"

"Watch this," Jeff said, and just like nothing he walked his ball out onto the pond and walked on water!

Chip and I were laughing like crazy now because Jeff had this very beatific look on his face as he walked across the pond, one arm raised perhaps to divide a sea if he had to and the other on his chest, and then turned and walked back the other way.

"Oh my gosh," Chip said. "This is going to be fantastic!"

Chip went to his ball, got in and closed the seal, and then started walking his ball over to the pond and Jeff was just smiling and waving.

"Pretty cool, huh?!" Jeff shouted, and I guess they had to shout. Physics you know, about sound not travelling well in a vacuum and all. And even though I was still laughing, part of me couldn't help but think that Chip and Jeff were the two best vacuums for several hundred miles.

Meanwhile I was getting pictures with my little pocket camera and trying to hold it still because I was laughing so much, because I thought this might make a pretty good column later on: "Dobbins Daredevils Devise New Distraction," or something like that.

And right when Chip and Jeff had discovered that they could bump into one another and send the other backwards, perhaps imagining a new form of bumper-cars, a bit of a breeze came up as Jeff was headed backwards from a bump by Chip, and started rolling him sideways. Suddenly he was off his feet and just getting rolled, and the next thing we saw was that he rolled off the pond, down the little slope, and disappeared.

Chip laughed and then walked his ball off the pond and eased his way down the slope and looked out.

"Al! Oh my god!"

And then he walked his ball off the slope and disappeared too.

I ran down the little hill and passed the pond and looked to see where they'd gone, but it didn't take long to see: on the other side of the pond was a maybe six-percent grade slope, and Jeff and Chip were on a two-mile ride down into Dobbins!

I ran back to Chuck, hopped in and yelled to him "To the Emerald City as fast as lightning!" or something similar. It might have been "Hi Ho! Silver, away!" but I don't remember. Anyway, we went as fast as we could.

We got on a parallel road in less than a minute, but Jeff and Chip were travelling faster than that for a while anyway, and so were still in front of us, and I could see them just absolutely careening down the slope and slowing only if one of them hit a big bump and sent the ball into the air, only to come crashing down once again on the slope with even more velocity.

I wasn't sure what I should do. Should I just try to keep up with them and when one of their balls got busted try to go over and retrieve the body? Or should I get Chuck to try to head them off at the pass? I asked Chuck about the latter and he explained, rather logically as he always does, "And then what?" Yes, there was that. No, I didn't have a gigantic volleyball net to somehow quickly erect in which to stop them. Chuck drove as fast he could, and I kept an eye on the bouncing balls, just following along.

I managed to get down into Dobbins just a little before Jeff and Chip did, and I could see that they were going to come down, amazingly, right on the holy-smokes highway which happens to be our version of Main Street. Chuck doesn't have a horn so I couldn't make any noise that way to warn people, and I just got out and ran down the street waving my arms and shouting "Get out of the way! Get out of the way!" if I saw a vehicle or a pedestrian.

Folks in cars and trucks just sort of looked at me and smiled, but I kept shouting and they slowed and I pointed, and their mouths dropped open when they saw two gigantic balls coming screaming down the highway, right at us. I had a momentary thought of trying to stand there and stop them, but reason kicked in and said that would be very stupid, and so I got out of the way and people in their vehicles closed their eyes as if the Apocalypse were on them, and why didn't somebody say so on the morning news and at least interrupt the report on what hay was going for.

Jeff and Chip, just spinning madly inside their balls, finally smashed into the Duds and Suds and came to a halt. We all ran over but I got there first. I knelt down to see how Jeff was doing and he groaned a bit but managed a thumbs-up. I got over to where Chip was resting a bit of a ways off, and he was still upside down, but he said, in just a little whisper of a voice "Wow. Wait'll we get our protective gear on, huh?"

Turned out, that was a really good column a few weeks later, and as I walked down the street I happened to see Chip on the other sidewalk, and he had a noticeable spring in his step.

CHAPTER TWENTY-FIVE:
I ASK MY THERAPIST A QUESTION

You may know that there are questions and questions. Some of them are harmless and occur every day. They're the things we define our lives and routines by. We ask ourselves briefly "What shall I wear?" or "What do I want to eat for breakfast?" and we're always asking. We're always asking after things. Oh, we ask after so many things. We seek out all kinds of things each day. We look to see at a weather forecast and if it might or not be raining for a child's soccer game. I look at the same things to see if it might or might not rain when I want to go fishing. I'm no different there. I try not to look at much else. I am afraid to. I don't want to be asking so very much. I am afraid to, and I'm not sorry to say so.

I told Linda, my therapist, somewhere in there, whenever that was, that I wanted to write something because I thought that might help. I said that whatever else we'd done I thought maybe I should try to say something else. I asked if she thought that was a good idea or not. She looked at me, right in the eyes like she always does, and said "I don't know. It could be bad, it could be okay. For awhile. You don't want to just keep forgetting and remembering, right?"

I have only just a little left before I have to stop. I told her that I would stop. She said that was a good idea, and I think she said that because I get everything all mixed up and I can't remember and then I just go back to where I was and we have to start all over again, and I am so tired now. So tired of trying to think things through and have an answer. Something. Just something to hold onto, some tether where at least if you reel yourself back in from time to time then you're okay. You're just okay. And that's good enough for me these days. It's just I can't remember, okay? It was yesterday. Or two years ago. I can't remember. I don't want to. I have to stop this now, do you see? This has to stop pretty soon.

CHAPTER TWENTY-SIX:
A BIT OF UNDERSTANDING

Sometimes the most I want out of anything, whatever it is, is just some basic understanding. It doesn't really matter what it is. It can range from "Why did the tree suddenly fall on me when it could have fallen ten seconds sooner or later," to "why are those stupid particle-board book shelves put together only in such a way that the translated instructions insure that you're going to do a whole bunch of swearing before you're done?" I think you know what I'm saying. The deal is of course that the things you most wonder about never end with someone just showing up on your front porch and telling you "You know that thing that's been keeping you awake at night? Well, I just stopped by to let you know that it's because of whatever the heck it is." Except if you're me. Except in just this one situation, and just this one time.

So, there I am mowing the "yard". I can't afford a lawn tractor and so just have my push mower and yes, I am going to mow five acres with it. I am going to do this not because I really care what five acres of grass really looks like to my neighbors, but rather so that I can have a pleasant bit of not thinking about anything whatsoever and also get in a bit of exercise. When you're walking a push mower, there really isn't any chance that you can coherently think about anything. You can't. You're just trying to stay in a straight line over uneven and bumpy pasture for whatever reason that no one can explain and that kind of takes up all your attention. Oh sure, you can think about things like baseball scores or dandelions, but that's about it. I love it. It's just sort of purging yourself of whatever it is that I suppose you needed purging of in the first place.

Anyway, that's why I didn't notice two kids on my back deck with their bicycles lying in the grass until I had made the north-south turn and began heading back toward the house, busily not thinking about any- thing. When I spotted them I had this very bad feeling that they were here for A Reason, and that my not thinking about anything was sadly going to be ruined. It was Morningstar and Thor and I could just feel something behind me, watching me, because that's just the way this world goes.

I made my final pass up toward the house and then shut down the mower. Morningstar and Thor looked at me and then each other as if they were unsure what to say, and so I said it for them.

"Hello. And what is the pleasure that brings you two all the way up here on your bikes?"

Morningstar stood, and then so did Thor, and Morn- ingstar sort of scraped the grass with one tennis shoe while she looked down at it, then lifted her head and said "We need to talk to an adult, and you're it."

Naturally, if you know me, I couldn't think of a darn thing to say.

"Really," Thor said. "Nobody listens to us. We keep trying to find ways to tell them, but we never can because they won't listen!"

Given that this was perhaps the most words I'd ever heard Thor speak, especially in the presence of Morningstar, I think I was just a little bit worried.

"Okay. Let's go sit down," I said, and pulled out lawn chairs so we could face each other. "Tell me, and let's see."

We did and then Thor said "It's because of my sister!" and Morningstar stopped him then with a look and turned to me and said "You don't understand. I need to tell you and tell somebody."

What Morningstar told me then was this:

After Einar and Siggi had arrived and bought up the ranches they thought they needed, Siggi was okay at first, getting away from the old house and its memories, and then thoughts of her daughter now past, her first-born and beautiful daughter, they couldn't let her be at peace. She told Einar that they should at least have some sort of memorial for Inga, their first, because of course they had had to leave her behind in Minnesota and that was very hard.

Einar agreed, and went looking. He found the most beautiful, tiny spring-fed pond on the edge of his property, all ringed with willows, and he brought Siggi to see it, and they both thought it was the most perfect place to set a stone, or a bench, or something, something just for them so that they could come when they wanted and remember little Inga. But it wasn't on their property. It was on the neighboring rancher's property. And that's when they met Jack.

He wasn't there. He was forty miles away looking after the rest of his concerns, and they were considerable. He had many mouths to feed that year, many men and their families to take care of, and they were all under his care and he knew it, and it weighed on him. It was a mighty responsibility to take care of all these people, but he and Haseya took it on willingly. But it was a burden. A thing you can't stop thinking about. So many people depending on you. All the work that must be done in just a few short months of summer, and everyone depending on it. So many things to tend to.

And that was why, when he got a letter from a neighboring rancher about selling just a small little tidbit of his land that Jack had summarily said "no". He didn't even read the letter fully but just got the upshot of it about someone wanting to buy a chunk of his land and he said "no". He couldn't think about anything other than all of his own concerns, as you might expect, and so he just couldn't think about anyone else, and what their concerns might be. That was all. Has that ever happened to you?

Thor said, "It's all about my sister, Inga. She was just two. She's dead. It was before I was born but I know what happened and why Mom and Dad came out here. And I know about why they're so mad at Morningstar's dad."

I looked at Morningstar and then at Thor, and back to Morningstar. I expected her to tell me what to do, but she didn't. She just looked at me. She's thirteen, you know, and I'm not sure what your experience has been with this, but when a thirteen-year-old asks for your help, then what are you supposed to do? And this was Morningstar Jackson for crying out loud!

I sat back in my lawn chair and looked them over. "Okay," I said, "but I can't do it without your help."

Morningstar stood up then, made a smart salute, all the concern gone from her face and said "Aye-aye Cap'n. When do we shove off?"

176

CHAPTER TWENTY-SEVEN:
FLORA AND FAUNA

Chuck and I decided that it'd be a good idea to get out of the house for a bit, given how things were going between Joanie and me, though I'm unclear what Chuck may have thought about this, and so we got up in the real-early and headed on out. I'd go ahead and tell you about this and that, but it's really all the same every time: Chuck is doing the driving and I'm drinking coffee and thinking about something, whatever it is that I might actually think about any longer.

We're just driving you see? We're just going somewhere and at the end of somewhere I will go fishing. I'll stand in the water again, and Chuck will have a bit of a nap or maybe he'll watch the birds and such which he often remarks about. It's always the same, for both of us. I sometimes wonder what Chuck likes so much. He's never actually said in so many words, but he likes this. I know it. Maybe it's all those little things that never get said, as people always say. It's just always the little bits in-between that really make for communication.

So anyway, we're headed off to the river, I don't remember which one, and as for myself I will stand in the water. It's possible that I have said or thought this or think I've said at some other point, but I just wanted to say something about the river is all, and again, it doesn't seem to matter which one it is. I'm not so sure any longer what had happened to me but in the river, where everything is always and never before, a beginning and an ending you can't see, because it's always all those things at once, rushing in front of you, then that's when I see again or either don't and am swept away to wherever it is that I must go.

I can't really explain that very well except to say that life for me is like the water, where I think I know where I'm standing, but what I see in front of me is past present future all at once, upstream, downstream, and straight ahead, and so "seeing" just depends on where you're looking at the moment. So, depending on where my attention is cast at the moment I might be seeing something then, now, and yet. Does that make any sense? Anyway, the only reason I'm mentioning this day at all is because of a series of surprises which seem to happen to me all the time anymore, either because I'm not listening to the in-between of a conversation or because I'm looking in the wrong direction. And then there are sometimes, just sometimes, when none of that matters and understanding wouldn't be possible for the best of us.

Let me just jump ahead a bit here and get a little closer to the point, which was of course the fishing and the river. This happened to be heavily forested canyon-lands and so I had to make my way down and down and finally down once again, walking through the deep-dark of the woods at that time. When I finally got down to where the river was, it was still all in shadow, almost still night-dark, just perfect I thought, and here and there I could stand in the rushing waters and not get too far out, even for a poor caster like myself who always wants to.

I had cast for some little time and caught and released a few fish when I decided to take a break and turned to the bank once again, and there was Kenna, of all people, in her waders and vest and holding her rod, sitting on a boulder. I laughed and waved.

When I got close enough I said "Small world, huh? How's it going?"

"Good enough," she said as I came close and also sat on a rock nearby. "Whatcha usin' there? Looked like a couple of good fish."

I showed her and she said "I got one of those," and rummaged around a bit in her vest, we all do you know, you never remember where all the little things might be that you think maybe you should have.

I sort of looked at my own vest for a bit then, thinking briefly about how I might make a car or an atomic bomb (pretty much) or a solar battery with what I had strapped to my chest and torso. Actually, I did have a small solar array in my vest, for my laptop, you know, just in case. I also had a couple of sandwiches in there somewhere, maybe in my back pouch I don't remember, and pliers and matches and several devices guaranteed to make tying on your fly a whole lot easier when you're a doofus like myself, and fly-line wax and fly ointment. There were matches and lighters and flint and a whetstone of all things, and of course my Lucky Rock.

I also had little fly-line pins in case I was too lazy to tie a leader to my line, and six boxes of flies when I only ever use two flies on any morning, if that, and a handy-dandy multi-tool that I'd gotten for Christmas one year which could pretty much do everything except wash your truck or do your homework, and yes, the solar array, kind of small, but still. I was kind of wondering as well where the sandwiches went, but I knew they were there somewhere. If ever I was lost in the mountains I was pretty sure I could live off the land for months with what I had in there, or else just build a satellite and broadcast my location.

While Kenna tied on a fly I had a chance to reflect, just a bit, on all I was carrying on my back and chest. I wondered: why am I carrying all this stuff around just because it's always been there? Why do I keep doing that? Maybe I should try to sort of, you know, thin things out a bit? I probably didn't need all those fly boxes and the multi-tool I hadn't yet used, and of course there was no way I'd be carrying a device that needed to be recharged, I mean, I don't even have a sort of smart phone. The lucky rock would of course remain where it always had, even though I no longer recalled why it was lucky.

Fascinating conversationalist that I am, based upon fifty-five years of reading anything and everything, ever since I could read by myself, I said "So, what's up? How you been doing? I haven't seen you for a month or so and I'm way overdue for my next haircut."

Kenna looked out at the river and said "Been getting along okay. Better every day. That's why I'm here."

Well, that was a relief because all I had to say was

"That's good to know, especially because I'm no closer today than I was a few weeks ago to finding him. I'm not sure what to do. I thought I did, and I even enlisted the help of others, but I'm almost, not yet quite, out of ideas. I have one left is all."

Kenna looked out the river and then back at me. "That's okay," she said. "I'm just getting on is all. That's what I'm doing right now, just getting on. Except I don't get up as early as you," she said with a half-grin.

"And now I am going fishing," she said.

Well, thank goodness for that, I mean all the way around, and so we meandered out into the current wherever it was we wanted to go, and Kenna was up above and I was down below, a good fifty feet or so. I remember that.

Kenna was up above and I was down below. I re-member this from somewhere but it's scrambled, all messed up somehow, it's the same thing from some-where sometime else, and I can't remember any better than that.

But I definitely remember, somewhere in that time-line, maybe after twenty or thirty minutes, that one of us looked over our shoulder, and Kenna and I have dif-ferent recollections of this, but whatever, it just didn't matter, because a male and a female Grizzly had come down the slope and had spotted us in their river.

You have no idea how fast they can go. You don't even have the time to say a proper prayer if you're fifty yards apart. No, that's your death coming, and it's going to be very violent indeed unless you're lucky in some way, maybe where your skull is smashed first and then you're torn apart and eaten later.

Kenna and I yelled at one another, and she started to head back to the bank for some crazy reason and I yelled and yelled at her to try to make her stop. I shouted as much as I could: "Stay in the water! Stay in the water!" because at least there you have a chance of merely drowning instead of being ripped to pieces, utterly savaged, and eaten alive.

Fifty feet. Just fifty feet and I could get to her and pull her back from the onslaught that she didn't yet recognize was going to happen. And there I was, utterly enshrouded in things: my waders and my boots that there was no time to remove, my vest, my vest so much in it just carrying it around for no reason at all so stupid, and I just couldn't get rid of it all! I couldn't dump all these things quickly enough to get to her, to at least bring her back into the water where at least we had a chance. Not a very good one, but at least a chance, just maybe live another day and see.

I waded as fast as I could, part of me singing backwards to at least the relative safety of the river, but I went forward for Kenna. Had to get her you see? All my fault. All my fault. Had to save Kenna somehow or Hollis or someone else I can't think about seeing now and I would never be able to speak them again. This was all my fault somehow and I had to get to Kenna.

These days it is difficult for me to know where I am or what I'm seeing. I know you can't understand that at all, and I'm glad for you. I'm only trying to say that when a tree somehow just suddenly detached itself from the woods and came down out of the woods with a very purposeful stride that I hope you don't give up on me right now. But it did. I'm not kidding.

A tree just came down from somewhere up above and went ahead and walked down to the river, where Kenna was still out, maybe fifteen feet or so, not so far I wagered in this water, not now, not right now, not so far out. And the tree stood in front of her and sort of waved its limbs I guess at Kenna and as you might imagine she held her ground where she was. The tree stood on the edge of the bank as the Grizzlies descended the slope and simply held out its branches toward them as if it were a traffic cop and waited

The Grizzlies had a hard time stopping their thousand-pound descent before they splashed into the river to eat both Kenna, and a bit later, myself, but you could just see them both, surprised, skidding on their butts because they wanted to stop and had no idea what they were in for, because I'm pretty much sure all of us never expect trees to tell us what to do, though they probably ought to.

The enormous bears, I'm guessing male and female, managed to come to a halt just a few feet from the tree that had suddenly presented itself, inexplicably, and the oh-so-much larger of the two decided he wasn't interested in surprises and started to move forward toward the tree when a shot went off! And then a juniper bush came sliding down the slope and before any of us had time to react, was somehow standing side by side with the tree, and aiming a very mean .38 Super at Mr. Grizzly. Right in his eye.

Mr. Grizzly looked the juniper bush up and down for several seconds and then reared on his hindquarters and roared, and that's a sound and sight you simply don't ever want to hear or see. It's fine on a film clip or something, but not when you're standing right there. There is no one on this earth, and I don't care who you are, who rules his world like a Grizzly does. Even the tree bent over a bit at that, but not the bush. This was one of those impenetrable hedges I guess.

Stacy stood her ground and fired two more shots at the big bear's feet and he roared again. But then he settled on all paws and turned, and his missus-to-be followed along, and they made some fast-time to somewhere else they wanted to be, and across the slope they went. After that, Kenna and I saw a tree drop to its knees, and so I guess they have them.

We both stood in the river, and looked at one another, but then the tree and the bush stood and the bush put an arm around the tree and just yelled at me.

"Al! You are becoming a serious impediment to my personal happiness! Dammit!"

The bush holstered its firearm with no small flare in doing so, given that it was a juniper after all, with no berries. Yes. I seem to have that effect on people, and even the landscape it seems. At least the bush didn't shoot me, and after catching its breath, the tree was just fine and stood straight as a, you know, as straight as a tree.

CHAPTER TWENTY-EIGHT:
CHANNELING HOLLIS

I'm guessing that since you've read this far and I've gotten to the point where I tried to explain that night with Hollis and an encounter with angels or fairies or magic or miracles or whatever the hell that was and you've been okay with that for some reason, or maybe you've just written that off to bad alcohol or something, but for whatever reason you're still reading this, and maybe it's just to see how Thor and Morningstar turn out, but you're still reading so I have to tell you this other thing. I'm just going to tell you this and whatever you think about it is fine with me.

So, Hollis left that night from my camp and then later I had a little bit of a visitation myself, or something, but anyway things changed then. They changed, whether for good or bad how can you know, but you sometimes are aware that something has shifted, just slid this way or that. Who knows? It happens I think. That happened is all I'm trying to say, but I can't say what it was. Anyway, later after Hollis went off and I fell into a deep sleep, I saw him.

I know. That doesn't make much sense but I don't have any right now so instead I will tell you that I saw

Hollis walk home. It took him two weeks. I can't have known this, I just can't of course. But I saw it, lying there on the cot in my tent. I saw every footstep.

I know of course that you can't believe this. Maybe it's because I don't understand time anymore. Maybe Hollis told me later and I only thought I'd remembered it. I hope you don't mind so very much that I'm kind of messed up a bit about all of this, I mean all of it, but let me just tell you, because that's the whole point.

So. He just leaves the campsite and I see him crash off into the underbrush, not at all like a former Army Ranger, and a lot more like some sort of zombie, because I can see his face and his eyes as well, and he is just walking in the most direct line to get to where he wants to be. It's like there's this demonic GPS system guiding him and just saying "that way." I think that's when I heard him splashing through the outlet stream to the lake that night, because I could see him, like I was on his shoulder, just marching across it because that's where he had to go.

Later, I see a campsite. It must be his. We have gone up and down and then finally up and up and he must be on some ridgeline somewhere. It's dark now and an hour until the moon can crest the ridge, and except for a few embers left in a fire-pit there is no other light. These are stomped on. I look down and see his boots wipe them out. There is a pack against a rock. It has a bedroll on top. He looks in it. There are several things that look like what I've heard described as MRE's. He has two large bottles of water. He slings the pack across a shoulder and walks into the night. There is a full moon now. It has just appeared. It obliterates all thinking. It just is, and its light is all there is. Everything else is shadow and ignored.

There is no path and I cannot see where we're going, but we're going no matter what. We slip through pines and firs and duck under branches and we stride over deadfall and we move, almost always in a straight line. We're very high up. The trees are mostly down below. We stride, we backtrack, we go forward, and we reach up and pull ourselves over rocks and downed trees. We go forward again. There is no stopping.

The moon has set and the sun is somewhere behind us, not yet visible. Hours have passed. We stop and drink water, and eat something from a can that has a pop-top on it. It is peaches or muffins or meat, it is hard to tell and is ignored. Hollis stands again, shoulders his little pack and looks around.

He sees that he has come to a point of impasse.

He stood and looked. He had come this way before, but it was light then and now it was in the still-dark before true light. We looked out, not knowing which way to go. A straight line was not possible. He had to find a road. We had to find some sort of road. Below was rock. To one side was river that couldn't be waded, crashing through a canyon. To the other side was forest that didn't go in the direction needed. We looked at the river.

We looked at the river and I said no but Hollis said yes and so we went. He stood at the river and I said no. We went into the river. It was dark and cold and had its own mind about what it should do and be, and it had no care whatsoever about anything else. It doesn't care about your past or your future because it is always these things all at once, and could never understand even if you could speak its language.

Hollis' long, strong legs waded out, and then there was no possibility of wading any more, and the river took him. Us.

I don't know what I'm seeing wherever it is I am, it is only a blur of images, but I am praying, no I'm shouting for Hollis to put his legs downstream so that we can ride what we can and not smash his head my head on the rocks below. We float above the stones. We slide between boulders. We laugh. We laugh! Ha! We are the river!

Just right up until we smash into a boulder and one of us isn't very conscious anymore but one of us has long arms and powerful hands and grabs onto a piece of log jam against the boulder and pulls us up and out and we are standing on a log soaking wet and there might be pain in places because Hollis looks down to check himself and he is breathing heavily but he looks up and there is a little purple-pink light dancing in the woods just maybe a mere fifty feet away and Hollis and I just as quick as anything survey the log and we are across.

We stop for now, head rested on pack, asleep. Dead asleep.

The next day was more. It was walking. There were trees and rocks and deadfalls and we are walking. Hollis is walking. He eats from time to time. He refills his water bottles when he can. But he is just walking. It's an easy sixty miles in a straight line to home and there isn't enough food or water or energy for that, but that's all he can think about. I see it on his face. I am along for the ride.

Days go by. The food is gone now but doesn't seem to bother him. Here is the road. It is not like the river because it just goes where it goes and it stops somewhere. It is not like the river. This is the road home. It is merely so-many-miles in that direction and then that is all. It is not an obstacle, it is merely where he must go, must walk. Where we must go.

Hollis sits down. He is so very tired. He has been worse off but that was when he was trying to kill the people who were very ardently trying to kill him. He does not think about that. He does not think about that time. He has a very firm wall up against then and now. I can see it on his face. I'm a bit proud of him for figuring this out. I think that I will ask him later how he has done this.

He hasn't eaten much and has just the one bottle of water to last him. He's thinking something that I can't see because it's in his head and I can only see what he's doing. We sit. We are so very tired. Beyond explaining.

Oddly there is joy or happiness or satisfaction or some feeling that I cannot feel because I can only see it on his face. I can't be there for that. I am not allowed. He is so happy. He can hardly even think. He looks at his boots and begins taking them off. He laughs! Hollis laughs! I tell him that this is a very bad idea because we have many miles to go and he tells me to go to hell and just shut up.

Hollis is barefoot, and will now walk fifty miles home. He carries his boots in one hand. Later he straps them around his neck. He walks. Days go by. He will stop and wander a few feet off the road to sleep. He is very tired, paying out what is left in him against a timetable that only he knows. He gets up in the morning and has a drink of water. He walks. A driver stops to ask if he wants a ride and he says no. He walks. Home is almost in sight. Another day maybe. He sleeps again.

And then I cannot see where we're going. I can't see anymore.

CHAPTER TWENTY-NINE:
CHUCK GETS ANGRY OR SAD OR SOMETHING

That next morning after I'd seen Hollis I got my things packed up as well as I could. Miraculously, I didn't even have a hangover. What I had instead was urgency. When everything had been packed away I got in and fired up Chuck then I kept saying "C'mon buddy, c'mon buddy, let's get down this mountain as fast as we can. There's something I have to do."

And you know Chuck, he's taking it easy in the switchbacks of course, but even in the little straight-aways he just seemed to sort of dawdle a bit, kind of looking at the scenery and just enjoying himself. I gritted my teeth the whole way down the mountain.

When we got down Chuck wanted to just go ahead and turn left and head north to home of course, but I yanked the steering wheel back over and said no, we're going south instead. Chuck, being the machine that he is of course just didn't understand this departure from what was entirely sound reasoning on his part.

"Listen Chuck," I said. "I haven't told you this before because I didn't want to upset you." I put my head on the steering wheel for a bit and then said "Go south. I'll explain as best I can along the way. It's important, okay? I've only just found out how important it is, or something."

Chuck idled a bit and then turned and south we went.

As we went south and away from home I scooted over and rolled down the far window because I suddenly needed lots of air, and then got back to where I was supposed to be driving because I thought that was probably a good idea because you know other people might be watching, but Chuck was driving so that was okay.

And then I tried, as best I could because understanding only ever seems to come on me like a lightning strike these days, to explain to Chuck what this was all about. It had been quite a few weeks since I last talked to him, and I merely thought of this as two friends being perfectly simpatico, but now, at this point, I realized I'd merely been hiding things from him. From me. I didn't want to talk or think about it, whenever it was in this timeline that I can't grasp any longer.

I talked and Chuck just listened. He's such a good listener. He's such a good friend. I told him that things weren't actually going well for me and Joanie and that we were mad a lot, and Chuck wasn't happy about that at all and kind of growled a bit, there's no other word for it, and I said that we just didn't understand one another right now, or so it seemed, and Chuck seemed to think about that and wondered how could that be? How could two people who'd known each other for almost as long as he'd been alive suddenly not know one another anymore? He thought that we always seemed pretty happy, and I told him yes, but you don't know.

I started to tell him something else but I didn't. I

wanted him to understand. I went back to the beginning, the shooting, the deaths, my best friend, my
nightmares, thoughts of suicide, how we lost Finn who
we loved so much and everything else, and you remember Finn? Little Finn? And Chuck knew. And I told
him how Joanie and I couldn't get along then, my fear
and broken head, the place where I'm supposed to
think about things but just can't quite a lot of the time.
I told him about my therapy and my lies and how we
had come here because of that, and wasn't that a good
thing because otherwise we'd have never met? I told
him about me and Hollis, and Chuck growled a bit
about that because he had never been sure about Hollis, but I reassured him that he was okay, just hurt in a
different way, and I told him about that too. I told him
of Maupsa, the cancer in her eye and our work on the
paper last year and chemo and standing on a cliff
ready to fall off or step back. I told him everything I
could think of, past present future. Everything I could
think of.

Chuck drove on, waiting for more. I told him about
the aftermath of the killing: my best friend, the river,
how I was broken and had tried to not be. Why I was
here. How I had run away, and I also said that I didn't
understand how to make Joanie happy any longer and
that he knew, he had to know, that happiness, in whatever way it comes to you, is all that matters. I told him I
didn't know what happiness was anymore, let alone
how to make anyone else happy, and because of that
everything that mattered to me was poisoned. Everything that should be the best things in your life was
now scorched and dying.

Chuck pulled over on the shoulder and then and came to an abrupt stop. He tried saying something, but he just couldn't. He couldn't , you see? He was so angry and confused and angry. He cried for a little bit, I could hear him, and I was so sorry I'd had to tell him all this. But I told him something green. I told him of the aspen grove and the green light and the Great Green Song. I told him. And I told him what had happened to Hollis and then later to me, just last night. And I told him what I had in mind and why, and he settled himself, pulled back onto the road where there was never any traffic, there were no other people, and sped southward, faster than he'd ever gone.

CHAPTER THIRTY:
SHOW-DOWN AT DEL'S

I sat at the crossroads, under the willow, and Chuck was a few steps away, resting in the shade of late summer. It was late in the morning, and on any other day at this time of year Chuck and I would have been returning from fishing in the mountains. But we weren't. We were just sitting, waiting for a change of some kind. Something was coming. It was time to go. Things had been set in motion and now it was time to go.

Some days just burn, all a-fire, while most of the time they don't it seems, and that's a pity, but there you have it. Sometimes you just have to wait for things.

It took Morningstar and Thor and I a bit of deception to get Siggi and Haseya at the Safeway at the same time, but it happened. What I mean, is, well, I told each of them to lie as best they could and make sure their mothers were pretty much there at the same time. Yes. That's what happened.

When Chuck and I pulled into the Safeway lot we strategically parked where Chuck could be seen, and of course everyone in the whole county knows who Chuck is. He's famous, you see? Thor and Morningstar had been instructed what to do after that. We waited. I briefly thought about dusting off the dashboard, or wiping Chuck's hubcaps, because I hate waiting so very much, but I didn't and just sat there.

You have to sort of picture this, but once I saw Morningstar and Thor come and sit on The Bench outside Del's, just for a dare, the two kids who shouldn't be together because their parents are in some sort of stupid feud, but there they were, sitting side-by-side on a bench, just waiting to be seen. They were nervous and wanted to hold hands for reassurance, but they didn't. Thor leaned over and whispered something to Morningstar and she laughed and laughed, but it only took the edge off. They sat and waited a bit, but then laughed together and got on their bikes and off they went. Oh, sometimes everything it seems depends on just sitting and waiting, and it's so hard.

Eventually I figured it was time and so I got out, and I let down Chuck's tailgate and sat there dangling my legs a bit. The plan was, well, the plan was to let the kids do the talking, that's what the plan was. I was only there as a meeting point.

I was close enough that when Haysea and Morningstar came out the front doors I could hear Morningstar say "Hey, Mom! There's that guy with the truck from the paper! Can we go see?"

That was step one, and step two followed shortly afterward with Thor and Siggi coming out of the Safeway and Thor saying pretty much the same thing.

My grand plan here was based on three important and basic truths: 1) kids can pretty much wheedle their parents into almost anything, especially if they're good kids like Morningstar and Thor, 2) women are, on average, a whole lot smarter than men in my experience, and finally, 3) women are on average smarter than men in my experience.

So, here came Haseya and Morningstar, and on a tangent here came Siggi and Thor. As the two parties arrived I got up off the tailgate and greeted everyone, and then before anyone could start to say this and that Morningstar and Thor jumped up and sat down on Chuck's tailgate and looked at their mothers.

"We have something to tell you," Morningstar said.

Without looking at one another, both Siggi and Haseya frowned at their offspring and Siggi crossed her arms and Haseya was just about to do so but she noticed Siggi had already done so, and so she didn't and had to stick her hands in her pockets to finish out what she thought was a serious look of disapproval.

"What will your father think?" they both said at once, and then looked sideways at one another.

I smiled. See? They already agreed about something.

Then Thor got down off the tailgate and stood, easily his mother's height at thirteen, and Morningstar did too. They stood close to one another, shoulder to shoulder, and Thor took Morningstar's hand and held it tight. He turned to Haysea then.

"We have to tell you something. It's important. It's something you don't know."

"It is Mom, and Thor and I are best friends and nothing is ever going to wreck that," Morningstar said.

Haseya and Siggi looked at their children and then Haseya first and then Siggi as well went and sat on Chuck's tailgate and I removed myself to the passenger seat and just sat and waited.

"So what's so important?" Haseya said.

"It's for me to tell," Thor said, and then added, "I'm sorry Mom, but just let me say it, okay?"

Siggi had no idea what in the world Thor wanted to say, but when he started talking about Inga and how she had died before he was born, she put her hands over her face and cried and Haseya looked over at Siggi and then put her hand on Siggi's arm, because as I've said, women are quite a lot smarter than men. What could she do otherwise? She knew this. Siggi had lost her little girl, and now her boy was all she had, just as Haseya only had her very special Morningstar.

Then Morningstar picked up the story about the final resting place and all and what had happened and why Einar was so mad at Jack, and then why Jack became so mad at Einar. And Haseya's mouth was open for a bit, and then it closed into a straight line and she looked out into the empty spaces of the parking lot, and then she absentmindedly patted Siggi's leg without looking at her. Morningstar had seen that look before, and smiled at her mother.

"It's okay Mom. We can still fix it."

Haseya looked at her child, and then at Thor. They still held each other's hands.

Haseya then stood and held out a hand to Siggi, who took it, still a little teary, and once they had both stood then Haseya gave her the bear-hug of her life. Which is saying something, given she's of course married to Einar.

They stood back and looked at one another and then they both wiped away some tears and Haseya said "Men," and that was all.

And that's when I came back and sort of reintroduced myself and explained to everyone the next part of the plan. And then everyone looked at me. I told them what I had in mind and everyone laughed. I am so simple and stupid most of the time that I think most people just want to see what might happen next when I get involved. They laughed, but I didn't.

A week later I made the short drive to Del's, left Chuck where I could keep an eye on him, and he me, and then wandered over and sat on The Bench. I won't reveal my thoughts at that time, whether I had any or not. I was not very happy I recall. I had no idea why in the world I had involved myself in this, but I had. No, I knew why I had. Morningstar and Thor. Of course I had to at least try. I waited. I wanted a certain kind of story. Who wouldn't?

Waiting waiting waiting we are always waiting. We want things to be and we wait for them. We look for love or solace or perhaps just a respite from whatever it is that breaks us and won't let us be at peace, and we wait; we're so very hopeful most of the time I think, and we wait because we have some sort of hope, even just a small amount of it, somewhere, just waiting. We never say that to ourselves of course. We never say out loud the words, the important words. Get up. Go on. Live. Find happiness somewhere. Just keep going, just another day and see what happens.

Now, I waited to see what would happen with my plan. I had enlisted Del in this, and she had set aside a large booth for my purposes. She had also enlisted, at my suggestion, about twenty people who would do what Del told them to do without complaining, except maybe Charlie, who always sat at the counter and wasn't going to change his ways: "No Ma'am, just to sit somewhere else to have this sannich after sixty years of sitting in the same gol' darn chair!" Charlie. What are you going to do? Everyone else was told to occupy every table.

I sat on The Bench. I waited. I don't imagine I mentioned the next part of my plan, which was also built on certain basic truths other than the ones I mentioned earlier. I'll try to mention them as we go along. Oh, and I had props. I'd never actually been in a drama before, but I brought them. I had my cup of coffee, and of course The Paper. I very intently involved myself in both of them.

Which is why I almost missed Jack and Haseya and Morningstar coming in for lunch, but I looked up briefly and saw them and unfortunately Jack had seen me too. However, given that this was indeed Gentleman Jack, he paused briefly, nodded, and said "Al."

To which of course I merely responded with the necessary nod and said "Jack. Good to see you again," which around here is all you need ever say to mere acquaintances, even if they're powerful ones like Jack. Haseya and Morningstar looked at me and quickly turned away, though Morningstar's left hand fluttered a bit, maybe in the code that she and Thor shared. I got back to my coffee and my reading because here came Thor, leading Einar and Siggi and they were on top of me in no time.

"Al!" Einar boomed. I stood and didn't really shake hands, but rather simply had my own enveloped by Einar's and said some silly pleasantries about this or that, and then Einar introduced me to Siggi and we also shook hands and she had some sort of giggle just about to come out of her and I almost did too and so I whipped around to Thor and said something, and Thor played the ideal thirteen-year-old and simply shrugged his shoulders and put his hands in his pockets, but I could see he was nervous. Einar and Siggi and Thor went inside. Oh Lord. Here we go.

I had earlier explained The First Rule of Men to Haseya and Siggi, an integral part of my plan, which is to never, ever lose face with another man simply because your wife/girlfriend is a much, much bigger person than you are.

Haseya looked at me and smiled. "Yes, this is so," she said, but Siggi wasn't so sure.

Haseya explained it to her, and gave several examples. Siggi laughed so hard she almost needed oxygen.

And that was why, after Jack and Haysea and Morningstar had been seated at the only table available, and then when Del ushered Einar and Siggi and Thor to the same booth, that Haysea stood up quickly before any words could be said by anyone else and greeted Siggi warmly and they both hugged and chatted about this thing and that and Haseya said oh, please join us, and everyone sat down. And they did. Thor and Morningstar sort of winked at one another. Kids.

Jack and Einar, stunned temporarily, did an anthropological dance of avoidance, which Gil could have much better explained than anyone, and looked at their coffee, their wives, their children, out the window, anything other than each other except for brief glances. Because this is what you do if you're a man.

Oh I know, you think you're supposed to lead and all, but you know darn well that just about three-quarters of your life you're trying to take a cue from somebody else, because you never, ever want to look like an idiot. That is just not a real good thing for anyone, but especially if you've been born male. And especially in front of your wife/girlfriend/significant other, or whatever. You know darn well that your wife is smarter than you are, and that's why you married her even if you didn't realize it, and there's no way you can just go ahead and admit it. Yep. Rule Number One was going well.

And so, finally Haseya said, "I was so sorry to cut you off the other day in the parking lot. You had been telling me about your little girl Inga and then my security alarm went off in the truck and I had to go fix that and then we just said goodbye. I would so like to hear more."

Einar sat up straight in the seat and looked squarely at Siggi, but Siggi, without looking at him, simply rested her hand on his own enormous one.

"Yes, she was our first and darling baby," she said and looked at Thor with great admiration. "We lost her you see..."

And then they talked just to one another, and Del had been instructed to not interrupt, and Siggi told the tale and then also about how they'd like to have a final resting place for their little girl, out here where they now belonged. Einar and Jack looked at their wives and Einar was getting teared up a bit, but Jack was enthralled with all this. He'd never heard it before, you see? All he saw was things like "justice" and "rightness" just as Haseya had shown him all along and which he embraced. And that's what he was hearing now. He was interested, despite himself.

Haseya said she knew just the place and described it and Siggi said we know exactly where that is and it would be perfect, and then Einar, because he briefly forgot the First Rule of Men, and given the circumstances I think he can be forgiven, said "But that's what I wrote in my letter to Jack fifteen years ago! That's exactly the place I suggested and he said 'no.'"

Jack sat there and looked back and forth at everyone. He looked at Haseya and she nodded. Jack looked at Siggi and then Einar.

"Oh dear God," he said, and they talked quite a lot more after that.

Thor and Morningstar had been talking to one another the whole time and had never stopped. From time to time they looked at the others and smiled knowingly at one another, but there was never really anyone else in their minds except each other. They reached across the table at some point and touched fingers.

CHAPTER THIRTY-ONE:
COMING HOME

Chuck went south as fast as he had ever gone. I felt, he felt I think, an urgency that couldn't be named. It was going to be a four-hour turnaround, easy, and then back up and down the mountains from where we'd come, and we wanted it all done. We wanted to be sure it was done.

That night with Hollis. That night when we were so drunk we couldn't see straight. That night when the lights descended on Hollis and not on me. That night when Hollis went away on some sort of quest that I don't understand, or maybe I do, but I'm no knight, only the jester, and the lights all spoke to him, but not me, and so I cannot know what they said to him.

I stood in the firelight for awhile, the embers down so much that I didn't worry about dousing them, and I really didn't worry much about anything I think, and I took myself into the tent and lay down on the cot, and there was a blanket at hand and I flipped that on my-self just a bit and tried to sleep.

I tried to sleep, but sleep and I are no longer on speaking terms it seems, and so I just lay there, empty, staring upward. If I hadn't had my eyes open then I probably would later think I was dreaming, but my eyes were open. They almost always are anymore, even when I can't see. I really don't sleep anymore like most people do I suppose.

I lay in the darkest dark that can be. There is no light for two-hundred miles, and it is the most singular place you can be. There is nothing else but you and a bit of nylon between you and the night, and all that it holds. There is nothing else for so far that you couldn't walk there, not for weeks. The stars are an easier destination, because at least you can see them. There's nothing here but the earth, the deep sighing of the trees and ground and stones and all of everything breathing out, that one last breath of day that they'd been holding in. And the lights appeared.

The lights were not multicolored as before, but rather only blue. They were a blue that cannot be said, and I will not try to say. And they did not dance or dally or dawdle or dissemble, and they came down from what airs in which they existed and sat on the end of my cot.

There is something going on with me that I can't understand. There are days when I am so frightened of things that might be that I don't do what I can or should. On other days, I see nothing at all and might walk in front of a speeding car because I just didn't see it. There are still other days when I see something, something somewhere, but I don't understand my perspective any longer: is it now? Was that somewhere in the past? Am I going somewhere I don't yet see?

The lights sat on the end of the cot. And then, one very, very small light fluttered into the air, a tiny butterfly of light, and came closer. It stayed pasted in the air just oh-so-close that it was just outside my reach. I slowly propped myself on one elbow as best I could and that was as far as I could go. I reached out a hand, palm up, and then I think I said please but I don't remember.

And the little light came closer, a tiny little thing of almost nothing, and it rested finally in my hand, and I fell back onto the cot into the deepest sleep I have ever had.

But I stand in the water. I rest on the rocks. I till the earth. I bend to the flowers. I touch their petals gently. The grass grows and I wade through it. The earth breathes all around me. Rocks and water, I don't understand where I am when I wake up. I only know that I must go, whatever time this is.

Fast.

I hope it is the present tense.

CHAPTER THIRTY-TWO:
HOLDING ON JUST ONE MORE DAY

I feel like telling you about a time when I was fishing. I was on a stretch of river that is fairly remote, which is to say that I was somewhere where no one could ever find me, which is pretty much the way I like things these days, and I was standing in the river and just casting, casting, and not really thinking about so very much I suppose.

I remember that I was watching an Osprey gliding down the river, silent as a stone, searching and searching and I watched and wasn't so much paying attention to anything else. I was just looking at a beautiful bird, gliding effortlessly and free as the wind, here in the lower airs, sleek as moving waters.

I think that was why I was so surprised by the sudden jolt on my line that almost pulled me off balance and into the river. I had a really, really good fish on and it was time to pay attention. I turned to lift my rod and my line against just a *zing* of line spooling off my reel, and then I found that I couldn't turn my right foot, the foot that would let me swivel to stand looking downstream to where I had to go, and I was stuck.

I tried to shift and lift my leg free, but my foot was stuck between two rocks and the current wasn't helping anything. I clung to my rod, and the fish was still on. I pulled back, playing the fish, reeled in line, and the fish ran again and I let it go. I couldn't watch very well because I had to look upstream, back to where I was in a sense because you always cast against the current, because I was stuck, and the fish was intent on going downstream, somewhere I couldn't go or even see.

I let the line play out again. I gave my foot a really good yank then, but nothing. I was really stuck. I wasn't going to get my foot loose. I held my rod in one hand and bent over as best I could and felt around in the water. My right foot was wedged between two rocks. I couldn't move the rocks. I tried.

Some minutes went by then, and I was getting tired. There would come a time when I would no longer be able to simply stand against the current. I couldn't get my foot free. There would come a time when I would no longer be able to stand. I would lie down and that would be it. I kept holding my rod. The fish was still on but I didn't really care about the fish anymore, or maybe I did, but there was no way I was going to abandon my rod and reel. Don't ask me why, because I won't tell you. You wouldn't believe me anyway.

The minutes went by. I yanked and yanked my leg against the rocks holding me until my ankle and foot ached. I was stuck. There was no way out. I stood there, doing nothing for a while. There was nothing I could do. I yelled a bit of something then and I don't remember what it was. I prayed a little after that.

This isn't how it's supposed to go. No one dies from having their foot stuck between two rocks. No one imagines their imminent death emerging from something as senseless and stupid as this. No one is standing in the middle of a river, with a fish on his line, praying that he might go back home just one more time. No, that's not how it should go for anyone.

I was so tired then, so very tired, and I pulled on my foot just the one last time with anything I had left, and it came free, it just came free. I turned and made my way back to the bank, stumbling but staying upright as best I could, with my rod in my hand, and when I had both feet on dry land with my legs quivering I felt a tug on my line, and the fish was still there. I reeled him in then, the both of us exhausted, and I know you won't believe me, but it was the biggest fish I have ever caught, just far and away bigger than anything.

He was alive still, and tired. I slipped the hook as gently as I could and took him back out in the current. I stroked him a bit and said some words of comfort as best I could, and he swam away, downstream, on his way again.

Chapter Thirty-Three: I Forgot to Tell You About George

I used to talk a lot about stories. All kinds of them as it happens because that's what my job asked me to do. I remember being an English major in college and my Mom and Dad hoping that one day I'd make something of myself and become a Dentist or Minister or, well, anything other than someone who just sits around all day reading things. You know, some sort of productive member of society.

I remember as well when I first discovered that there were actually jobs that would pay you to read and talk about stories to other people. They didn't pay you very much for doing so, and oddly you had to spend enormous amounts of money to get one of these very few jobs, but really, who could blame them? At times in my life I've imagined myself homeless and have been on the cusp of that a couple of times, and I could just see myself on a street corner with a little sign that said "Great Literature Explained: One Dollar!" So, that's what I set out to do, and I guess you get what you deserve in this life. Anyway, all I'm saying is that I have to tell you a story. I'm not getting paid for it this time, so you're okay.

I hadn't seen George most of the summer, but that wasn't particularly unusual because it was summer, you see? In summer, when you can actually live out here, then you live every moment like it might be your last. There's no time to just mess around and there's no such thing as "boredom", because everything has to get done during the summer. Everything. You try not to sleep very long if you can help it, maybe just a few hours, because it's all out there waiting for you. You can't miss a second of it.

Besides, this was when I was usually out fishing or hiking with Joanie, and this was also George's busiest time of year too. Once, when I was ambling down the street in town I passed his shop and instead of the usual sign he always kept on his window this one said "Out of town. Back in two weeks." I figured maybe he'd gone ahead and visited those family members he said he couldn't stand after all.

Anyway, one morning in late summer I was sitting at the counter at Del's, communing with my second cup of coffee, when a hand came down on my shoulder and there was George.

"Hey Al. How ya doin'. Got a minute?"

"Hey George," I said. "How's it goin', sure."

"Let's get a booth in the corner, okay?" and he grinned a bit.

After we'd relocated into the recesses of the diner and sat down I said "Boy, it's been a while since I've seen you. Looks like you're letting your hair grow out some too. It looks good."

George pulled on his relatively short ponytail and said "Yeah. Been letting it go this summer."

"So you've been busy this summer then? Haven't seen you around."

"Al, you know that whole business about me not wanting to be Cherokee any more just so people don't like, I don't know, have all these kind of crazy expectations or something? Remember you said 'Greek' and that I should go home and look it up? Well, I did."

"So then what?"

George leaned forward and put his elbows on the table and told me.

He said the first thing he did when he got home was get on the internet and look up "Greek Men", which turned out to be a bad idea because he either got crazy dating sites or else photos of male models from Greece wearing blousy white shirts with gold medallions hung on hairy chests. After that, he decided he'd just learn things about Greece itself, and he said he spent just about every waking hour reading up about Greek history and tourist places, and small picturesque villages, and remote islands with even more remote villages, and ouzo and crazy-sounding cheese and anything else. He even found a tourist site where it taught you how to say a few phrases in Greek, and you could listen to the pronunciations and everything and he said them again and again because, he said, it just sounded so cool to say, you know?

Anyway, he said he thought the whole Greek thing was crazy, just as crazy as not wanting to be Cherokee any more, but he really enjoyed learning all the things about Greece and started to do some research about what it would take to visit there. He said that he saw pictures of this one little island called Therasia, which was supposed to be very quiet and had all those beautiful white-washed buildings like you always see in pictures of Santorini, and he started looking into it.

"It is the most beautiful place I've ever seen," he said. "I just knew that someday I was going to end up going there. You know, after I've saved up a bit and all."

So, then he said that one day in June not so long after we'd had The Conversation here at Del's, three young ladies came into his shop, which was only sort of open at the moment because George had just had a delivery of things and was moving the boxes inside. The three women found him outside his door hauling things in and said that they had an interest in horses and could they come in?

George said, "And you should have seen them too! I mean they all looked like they're out of calendar photos or something, and they're all laughing and nudging each other, just having a great old time. So heck yes I told them they could come on in and tell me if they saw anything they liked. I mean, you know, you're not too old to understand that, right?"

I assured him that I was not. George went on to tell me that these ladies looked as though they had money, obviously being tourists, and he was just about to do his best "Cherokee" sales-pitch (which made me think of Daffyd at the fly shop, and why his blasted Scottish accent is so persuasive) when he thought he noticed something about how the women were talking to themselves as they went through his shop. They're speaking Greek to each other! He'd heard it. He knew how it sounded! These ladies were from Greece! He could ask them all kinds of questions about Greece!

Except he didn't, because when one very pretty woman came to him with a question he met her with a respectful greeting phrase in Greek that had just popped into his head. She paused just briefly and then smiled.

"You speak Greek? Out here in the wilderness of America?"

And then George said he was looking at her and he got all confused and figured maybe this was his big chance (though I'm still unclear about what), and he said he got kind of tongue-tied or something and he couldn't figure out what to say, so he said: "Oh, my family is from Therasia."

George stopped for a minute there and finished his coffee. He looked over at me and said, "It's this amazing little island. It's all I could think to say. But it gets even better from here on."

So George told me that the woman, whose name is Alessandra and who goes by Alex, started to ask him all kinds of questions about that tiny little village where his family came from and that she had never visited there before, and George said that he didn't know what to say because he was kind of just looking at her eyes and hadn't really noticed before that people, especially women, had, well, you know, these eyes? So he said that oh, his family had now lived here in the States for quite some time but he remembered enough details to say this and that about the island village.

Alex smiled at him and said how wonderful and why was he here in the middle of frozen mountains and endless wilderness? And George said he had come here for the adventure of it all and to find himself and to be at peace with the world. And Alex smiled a smile that George had never seen before and which made his legs wobbly.

"I don't know Al. It was like the colors of a sunrise painted across my mind or something." He looked out the window.

"Oh brother," I said. "I think I'm getting the gist of this, and because I'm thirty years older than you, you'd better darn well tell me the ending or I'm going to scream."

So, then he told me he found out that these three were headed over to Glacier and were going to do some hiking, and that this was their big three-month vacation and they'd decided they'd see some Real American Wilderness and George got out a map and sat them down and told them where they should go and what to see and also to talk to his friend who worked the train there and to just mention his name and so on.

They were all so very pleased with all this, but none so much as Alex, and as he handed her the receipt for the few little things they'd purchased as mementos she held his fingers briefly and smiled and said goodbye in Greek.

"I just about fell down right there," George said, "but you know, I'm Cherokee. We can take anything."

George said that two weeks went by and once again he was down at the shop because some crazy tourist wanted to get her tack from him as opposed to the Coastal, because she knew it was superior because it was obviously cared for by a Native American, and "real" people such as he wouldn't mess about with substandard gear. George was just about to say that his people really weren't all that into horses per se, and while he was at the University of Oklahoma for his Master's degree in History that he understood that the whole "horse-thing" was kind of later with the Spanish and was sort of biting his tongue, when Alex walked in.

When she did, George turned to the woman whom he was dealing with and said "It's all free. Really. You strike me as someone who knows what they're talking about, and I'm impressed. You need this more than I do. I'll bring it right out."

The woman was of course stunned, but somewhere in her mind she attributed this to her own breeding, race, station, wealth, gender, status, being in foreign parts where they do things differently, acumen or whatever, and so that was okay, because she left and went out to her car, and that was all that mattered. Because Alex had walked into the shop, his shop, in the middle of nowhere, and George hadn't slept in two weeks.

"You're right," I said. "This is getting good."

So George said he was trying to make his mouth work in conjunction with his head, which hardly ever works, trust me on that, and the best he could manage was "Hi Alex, it's great to see you again. Are your friends here with you too?"

Alex said, "No they've gone on to Yellowstone now. That's our next stop."

"Oh, so you're headed off to meet up with them then. But, uh," and George shoved his hands in his pockets, "I hope you don't mind my asking 'cause I'm really glad to see you again, but why aren't you with them?"

That's when Alex ran her hand over a couple of saddles and looked kind of intently at them and asked

George if he wanted to come and show them around and that they had booked three rooms at the lodge. George paused there and looked out the window, then back at me, then out the window again and said he was just sort of stunned at that and then went over to his computer and typed out a new sign to put in the window and showed it to Alex.

"That's perfect," she said.

So, George cleaned out his truck a bit, grabbed some clothes and such and stuck them in his duffle, and then he and Alex headed over to Yellowstone and they talked for hours on the way.

George looked up from his coffee then and said "I think I'm going to just skip those two weeks because I know you are very old, almost a tribal elder if you had any wisdom which I haven't yet seen, because I don't want you to have some sort of infarction or something." He grinned, and if I can say so of a friend, it was a wicked one.

"You show her the geysers there I'm guessing?"

"That the best you got?" he said.

"Sorry. Please go on."

And he did. So, yes, he showed the girls around and you can just stop right there if I can't call females girls if they're forty years younger than me, and they all had a great time. But, the time was getting on and the three Grecian ladies were due to head south now to Zion before they had to head back to the coast and do a trip south for a bit and then get their flight out back home.

"But here's the thing, Al. One night after dinner we were back in her room and she asked me am I really Greek?"

And George said he was just about to say something about that dreamy little island village again, but he just couldn't and so he said no, he wasn't, and the only reason he did was because he had this crazy friend who was a little bit off and that his friend said he should maybe try to pretend to be Greek. He said that Alex thought that was really funny and I was just about to amend George's memory of all this when he said that no, that wasn't right. It was because of this, that and half a dozen other things which he went on about for five minutes and then said that he was actually Cherokee. You know, Native American and everything. From Oklahoma and all.

He said Alex was kind of quiet about this while he went on about whatever it really was that was bugging him because I can't imagine what it was, and that she finally stood and said "I thought so. You're one of the First Peoples here. How cool is that?"

George had now finished his coffee and was sort of playing with the mug, looking at it, into it, around and by it, and then said "You know what I said before right? About not wanting to be, you know, Cherokee, right? Well, that's all done. That was just some stupid thing brought on by thinking about too many other stupid things, and I can't believe I let that silly woman take my stuff for free that day. Anyway, that's all done. I just wanted to say thanks for getting me thinking about Greek is all. Alex is renting a place here in town for a while."

I was just about to say something like "What?" when George stood and said in a stage-aside voice: "There she is! She's here! I want you to meet her!"

And so I did, and learned yet another of life's glorious stories. It's just the way things go sometimes. You never know.

CHAPTER THIRTY-FOUR:
WALTER AND VERONICA GO ON HOLIDAY

William Wordsworth once said that we all of us spend our time doing meaningless things as part of our routine, instead of just not doing that and living the life we really wanted to have. Naturally, he said it quite a lot more eloquently than I can, but that was the upshot of it. I think about this from time to time, and how I may waste my days doing meaningless things. Even so, I know there are plenty of people who do very meaningful things, all the time, and can never just seem to get away from it.

I recall that it was early June and so summer had just now come upon us, and I was down at The Paper just sitting around talking with Chip and Jeff, who had made some plans to go on a week-long fishing trip over on the Missouri, where they hadn't been for years. I'd had to turn in two columns that week, just so that they could have two issues coming out and still get away for a week. It was worth it. Chip was so excited he could hardly stand waiting a couple more days until they left.

"We haven't gone there since we were kids and Jeff caught that enormous brown trout. I think this time I'll get the Big One. It'll be great. It's way out and up there. We've got our campsite reserved for the whole week."

Jeff was equally excited.

"We're taking the Balls too," he said. "We're going to float the river at some point like no one has before. It's going to be great."

"Really?" I said, "You're going out on the river with them?"

Chip said, "It's just going to be great. I can't wait any longer."

Jeff pulled a tackle box from under his desk and opened it, and we spent the next few minutes admiring all the new lures he'd bought.

And that's when Walter walked through the door, for the second time in six months. We all looked up, a bit confused maybe, perhaps a bit apprehensive. The last time he'd walked through that door, which had been the very first time, was not a good thing.

"Hey guys," he said. "I was just coming to see if it was too late to get something put the Announcements for Saturday's edition?"

"No, we can still do that," Chip said. "What's up?"

"I've decided to take Al's advice and take Veronica on vacation. Just the two of us. For two full weeks. Veronica's Mom and dad said they'd be happy to look after the kids and be grandparents now."

Jeff and Chip cheered, and I sighed in relief.

"That's really good," I said and came up to Walter and shook his hand. "Where will you go? I mean, you know, unless you don't want anyone to know."

Walter laughed. He laughed!

"No, I was going to mention that in the announcement as well. You know, just in case somebody needed me real bad and so they could have my speed-dial where I wouldn't pick up."

We all whooped at that! Ha! Walter and Veronica on holiday! It sounded like a movie.

"But really, I've got a cabin for us up in Glacier, and then we're headed out of the country to Banff for another week."

"Wow," Chip said. "That sounds almost as good as what Jeff and I have planned. You know, without the beautiful wife and all," and then he looked sort of stricken about that and said "That's not what I meant at all! You know what I mean!"

And we all just laughed and laughed.

Walter pulled his announcement for The Paper from his pocket and handed it to Chip, and we all shook his hand and said things and he slapped us all on the back and we were so darned happy for just a little thing. Just this one little thing. How nice is that? Sometimes everything goes just the way it should in a story, just every so often, and you shouldn't take those little bits for granted.

Of course we did ask who would be law enforcement in the area when he was gone and all Walter said was "Got it covered. College buddy of mine. Travis is from over in Missoula and said there'd be cover, because Travis' never been here before and wanted to see what it was like. That'll be Sergeant Travis to the likes of you," he said with a grin.

"And don't you dare let anyone give the Sergeant a hard time, okay?" Walter said as he went out the door. "That's a real close friend of mine. Coming over for a few days before we go, just to kind of get oriented a bit."

As it happened, when Sergeant Travis pulled into town in a black truck with the tricked-out strobe lights behind the grill and the blacked-out windows, I happened to be sitting on The Bench at Del's and Walter and Veronica had just pulled up in another part of the lot and had gotten out and had seen the truck as well. A number of guys had already gathered around the truck because it was, well, you know, a very cool truck. It's largely a guy-thing I guess, but obviously not exclusively. Anyway, about five guys were just sort of giving the truck a good once-over in their sheer admiration, and that's when Sergeant Travis got out.

Sergeant Travis stepped out, six feet tall, and shook out her long blonde hair. She was, well she was, you know what I'm trying to say okay? She was not anyone's idea of what "sergeant" was supposed to look like because she was unusually beautiful, okay? I can't believe you made me say that.

The guys who'd been admiring the truck now stood back, several paces, unsure what to think. What I think is that admiration merely shifted. I think their mouths were open.

Veronica saw her before Walter did and she ran across the parking lot.

"Emma!" she called, and at that Sergeant Travis whooped and ran to her and they collided in a bear hug, each one lifting the other off the ground by turns. I stood and like pretty much everyone else in attendance watched with a smile. "College buddies," Walter had said. Looked to me like it was really Veronica's college buddy and not his. And the two of them stood in the parking lot for ten minutes talking before Walter even moved. He knew this apparently, and just stood back and smiled. Then he walked over to where Veronica and Sergeant Travis were standing.

Veronica turned and laughed and shouted "Walter! You didn't say Emma was your replacement! You didn't say!" and she laughed and held Emma's hand.

"Just a bit of a surprise is all," he said coming up to them both.

He held out his hand to Emma and she smiled and shook it.

"Great to see you again Walt. Nice place you got here it looks like. I could get to like it, you know?"

Walter smiled again. "It's so good to see you two to-gether again after so long." He turned to Veronica and said "And she promised to stay a week after we get back so you two can get caught up again, and so you can buy her T-shirts and tourist stuff at Glacier," and he laughed.

Sergeant Travis, and Walter and Veronica too, went into Del's for breakfast of course, and Ricky ran two miles to find nasturtium flowers to put on the sergeant's number 6, in-between taking orders. I guess he has this deep interest in law enforcement, you know, between Stacy and now officer Travis. Who knew? And, well, maybe a few of the rest of us just sort of, you know, thought maybe it was time for another cup of coffee and went back in too. You know. Just be-ing sociable and all.

After The Paper came out on Saturday everyone knew who Sergeant Travis was and why she was here and of course also the fact that Walter and Veronica were going to go away, all by themselves, for a full two weeks. And, as very nice a person as everyone discovered Sergeant Travis was, not to mention it was pretty clear to everyone seeing her and Walter go around town that she absolutely knew what to do with her .38, and also packed pepper spray and a taser, "just for fun" she said to someone who asked, there was still a bit of uncertainty and consternation about Walter actually leaving us, you know, kind of all on our own and everything. You have to understand as most of us had not until it was time for him to leave that we came to understand we had sort of taken Walter for granted all this time and never knew it.

Walter was Law Enforcement here, and everyone knew that of course, but it was more than that. Walter would never know this because no one had ever bothered to say it to him before, but he was trusted and understood and relied upon in a way none of us ever really appreciated until it was time for him and Veronica to take a simple two-week vacation. It made some of us, well, kind of nervous. "But what if..." some of us thought, and "What would happen if..." others began to ponder.

When the day came for Veronica and Walter to head out of town, quite a few of us had unknowingly and unofficially gathered on what we think of as Main Street, which of course is just 81 as it comes through town and you slow a bit, to see them off, you know? Just a sort of casual gathering which never, ever happens here, no matter what. When Walt's truck came down the street it was kind of a one-vehicle parade of sorts.

Walter's truck was all packed as we could see, with a canoe on top and the whole back bed bulging with stuff and covered in a tarp. We all just sort of stood there as if we just happened to be there and then finally somebody waved and then the rest of us did too and then, I don't know, we were all shouting stuff at them like "Have a good time!" and "Watch out for Grizzlies and don't forget to hang your food in a big tree!" and "Watch out for rattlesnakes!" and well-wishes like that.

Walter slowed and came to a stop and we crowded around. He leaned out the window and we all kind of came up one by one to say a little something.

Josh from Kendall's drug store came up and said "Heard there's some poaching going on, on the other side of McMasters of all places. Six elk taken and all."

Walter's face went sort of blank and then somehow focused again.

"McMasters?" he said.

Veronica frowned, put her hand on Walter's arm, and leaned over to look past Walter and said to Josh, "Thanks Josh. Tell Stacy okay? That's her job."

Walter turned to her and smiled. "Of course," he said. "Ha! Stacy's the best there is. No worries there, for sure."

And then there was someone with one of those so-called "smart phones" who came up and said goodbye and well-wishes and all the while still looking at his stupid phone, and said "Walt. You've probably seen this already I guess, but there's a big pile up on I-90 in the fog. Maybe sixty vehicles it looks like. They're asking for help."

He handed his phone to Walt who said "Damn!"

Veronica yanked on his arm and he looked at her again.

"Right," he said, and handed the phone back.

Yet another woman came up and said how much they'd both be missed, but couldn't help but remind Walter of the fire going right now, just forty miles away, and who knew if the wind might shift?

Walter gritted his teeth and smiled, looked over at Veronica, and saw her look. What could he do? Everyone needed him. How could he break Veronica's heart?

And then Maude appeared. So-small Maude, who I'd known now the past two years as one of the members of Kenna's audience and one of Dobbins' oldest matrons. She came, not to Walter's side of the truck, but rather Veronica's. She stood with her cane, wavering just a little bit, and rested herself against the door of the truck, and both Walter and Veronica turned to her. She leaned down, just a bit more, from tiredness or age or both, and Veronica held her hand on the window sill.

"I simply wanted to say have a good trip as well is all," she said with her tiny voice.

She cocked her head sideways then and said "Do you hear me at all Walter?" And Walt had turned and said that of course he had.

"Listen," she said. "How many children have been born in our town in the past five years save your own?"

"One," Veronica said and Walter nodded.

"That's right," Maude said. "But listen Walt, I know how important you are to all of us even though we never say it, but listen. To our little town, to most of us, your wife and children are the most important thing to ever happen to us. Don't you ever forget it. We need all of you, you see? Veronica needs some time to get away just like you do," she said very seriously.

Then she began to get upright, but before she did she said "Wait 'til they're two!" and she laughed and said, "Get out while you still can," and straightened and walked back across the street.

Walter cleared his throat a bit and said "Thanks Maude."

And that's when a big black pickup rolled down the street, with blacked out windows and just an attitude radiating from it. Out stepped Sergeant Travis, and swept her hair out and snugged down her patrol hat. There was almost an audible "Ooooo" from the crowd.

I think about fifty percent of us then looked away from Walter and Veronica, perhaps somewhat more if I read expressions correctly like I used to.

Travis sauntered up to Walter's truck, said a couple of words, and then turned to the rest of us.

"Let's get this street cleared shall we folks? Tourists comin' through before we know it."

And if Walter was Law around here, there was no way in the world anyone was going to argue with Sergeant Travis. Not on your life.

Walter and Veronica drove off into the sunrise, just as the story should go.

CHAPTER THIRTY-FIVE:
THE GREAT HAY BALE CELEBRATION

The day came. The earth had shifted once again, and all you had to do was look up to know it. Here, in little Dobbins, you need only to look out your front door to tell you all that you might ever need to know. Here there are no great questions weighing on your soul. Here, there is only sky, and grass and the impenetrable mountains that circle and define your life.

It was late August now and the world was going its way as it always does. You only needed to look up to know. The blue of the sky was no longer the blinding-blue of mid-summer, and had softened to a paler, perhaps softer sky, something now being given up and spent. The clouds, once gigantic that marched across this open land just weeks before, here where clouds and sky rule at almost all times, were somewhat worn themselves, giving away to something else, just a rag-tag band of the sky's warriors, all coming home now, weary of the days. We all knew it, and had seen it before. This was the gentle time before the great sleep and rending and reckoning of winter, and all the other changes to come.

The gods had gathered it seemed, but now, just now, there would be no thunder, no threats, no further conflicts of sky and earth, but rather a sky that had worn itself out over a long year, and resolved itself to itself. The skies looked down and were pleased. Earth and sky looked at one another, so long divided, and were reconciled in this brief time.

We all came, all of us, the whole town was invited. We came, even more than who had come for the sled race. We came to the nexus of where the dispute had first started. It was a very long drive, but nobody was going to miss this. We came to that place because we had heard about the Great Feud that was now to end.

I wish I could say, really say, what it was like: to see and describe everything, but I'm just one set of eyes and ears and poor words, and so I can only do so much for you.

We came to a small space where there was a quiet, spring-fed pond, ringed by the elder trees in attendance, and we had all parked a long ways away and had hiked up, and even though there were so many of us, we were very quiet. You could tell where you were. This was a holy place. It was a resting place. A sacred place. Round bales and square bales made a half-ring in the background behind the pond where the gods had stilled the waters. We noticed.

We stood around, waiting, because Einar and Siggi and Jack and Haysea were there at the pond, in front of it, and Einar had a large iron bench in his arms, much heavier than anyone else could hold, and he just stood there with it in his arms, and Siggi had her arm around him, or at least half of him, and Jack and Haysea stood off a bit. And Einar told us what we had come to hear.

Einar began: "Today, today we come to put our little

girl to rest so that we can remember her properly as we please." And he set the bench down.

"We had to leave her behind when we came out here to be here for good, but we came anyway. We came because we couldn't stand it there anymore, in the shadow of our little girl."

Einar stopped and looked at Siggi, and she nodded. "We have come," and Einar's enormous voice dropped so much that we moved forward to hear better, "so that we may all have peace. All of us. We think this is the best place for her, and so I made this little thing to set here, so we might come out from time to time and remember her. She was," and Einar had to stop again, "a very, very bright flame and we miss her so much."

Einar paused just a second but I looked over at Jack and Haysea and while Haysea's face was straight and resolute, seeing an end she knew needed ending, Jack's head was turned down to the earth, and he had a look of remembering I think, if that's an expression a person can have.

Einar said "In this place we think we want to have a remembrance of our little girl," and Einar was struggling now with words, this giant of a man, but Siggi's hand was on his arm and that's all he needed in this world, and so he carried on.

"We found this place when we first arrived," and he glanced quickly to where Jack stood. Jack's head was turned downward still, just looking at the earth.

"And we knew that it was the perfect place for her," Einar said.

"We are," and he struggled with his huge voice again, "so very happy. We are so happy for Jack and Haseya's gift of this place to us, and all that it means to us and our little girl. And..."

But Einar was so close to tears now that Siggi's arm somehow wrapped itself around him and he was quiet now.

And in the quiet that followed Einar looked down at the earth, and back at the pond, and down at the bench, and Siggi squeezed his arm a bit and he looked up at her and smiled and then he straightened and said "We're so happy we could bust!"

Holy moley. We cried at bit then, collectively, and then what the hell, a big cheer came up and Einar stood straight again and even though this was a solemn moment we were all so happy!

Einar turned, because it was his to say what happened, and then...I'm not sure how to describe everything all at once. Jack strikes me as a, well, sort of intellectual person who sees everything and takes care of business in the same way, I mean, you know, for a rancher who has his strong hands dirty at the end of each day, but I'm unclear about what his thoughts might have been when Einar strode across the green-green grass in front of that pond, just-so-many-feet away, while Jack saw him coming and perhaps for once in his life didn't know what to do next, and Einar said "Jack!" and embraced him in the only Grizzly-hug you might ever live through.

And when Jack was returned to the earth he looked up at Einar and took off his hat.

"I am pleased, and my wife is pleased," he said.

Einar stood there, smiling down at him. "May we be friends then?"

And Jack said "I'd be more than happy. I think, I think I'd be, well, you know even more than happy about that." And he laughed.

He laughed! And Einar laughed! And Einar was just about to hug him again when Jack stepped a bit back to protect his ribs of course, and Einar held out his hand.

"This is so good," he said.

And that was that.

Off in another meadow a huge feast had been laid out, and many picnic tables were spread. Jack and Haysea's family, and all of Einar and Siggi's folks were there, and we all sat down together, just looking each over at first and then smiling we all sat down where we could. And we ate. We told stories and laughed. We laughed to be alive, and to be living, right now, on this day.

But Thor and Morningstar went off by themselves and found a table to be alone, but they weren't, because almost all of us were watching them, because of course they were something out of a story that everyone seemed to know. We all knew the story, whichever one it is, but you never know how it will turn out. You want to watch and see, because you can never give your attention to just one story, because if you do, you'll miss the other ones. You never know.

They sat and talked quietly, eating the fried chicken and potato salad, and then Thor said something and Morningstar laughed and laughed and her hand slid to the center of the table where they sat across from one another, and Thor's did too, but they didn't quite touch. And we watched them, we all did. It was a story and we had to see how it was going to go.

At some point Jack and Einar went off by themselves and found a quiet table. They sat across from one another.

"Quite a day," Einar said, and sat his beer down on the table.

"It was a beautiful day," Jack said, and sipped his wine.

They sat there, each looking sideways at something, and then Einar said, "I don't know why I'm saying this because they're both just thirteen you know, but they seem to really, really like one another..."

"I think they more than like one another," Jack said. "To tell you the truth I've never quite seen anything like it."

They both turned to where Thor and Morningstar sat, and they both smiled.

"Have you ever thought what would happen if they got married?" Einar said, looking away at something.

"It'd be like they were royalty," Jack said, looking down into the swirling wine of his glass, perhaps scrying the future, "except they'd be joining two royal families together."

Einar turned and looked at Jack. "Wouldn't that be something? I mean, wouldn't it?"

Jack looked up at Einar. "It really would. It would be amazing."

They stood and shook hands, smiling at one another. "Will you keep an eye on...?" they both said together, and then laughed and slapped each other on the back.

Some ways away, Haseya and Siggi were watching.

Haseya said "That didn't take as long as I thought. I'm surprised at Jack. He's a good man and all, but not as quick as I maybe give him credit for."

Siggi just watched. "That went well, don't you think?"

"Very well," Haseya said.

Siggi and Haseya turned and looked at where Morningstar and Thor sat, and then turned again at the same time and simultaneously said "Would you mind keeping an eye on..." and then they laughed and laughed.

I actually saw all this. I turned at last away from it. I went and found a picnic table where no one was sitting. I sat and looked down, and very quietly, just to myself because you never know who might be listening, and with a tiny smile I said in just a whisper of a voice, "Hoka hey!"

CHAPTER THIRTY-SIX:
A CHAT WITH MORNINGSTAR

I'm almost certain that somewhere along the line I was telling you about how I sometimes get confused about things, or maybe about how I just don't see things like I used to, and I'm not quite sure I even know what I mean about that. Whatever it is I think maybe it's because I don't understand people and the world I live in the way I used to. You think you know something and then you find out you don't.

I thought I knew Gil well enough, for example. I thought I knew and I didn't. I never saw it coming, I never saw it and I guess no one else did either but that doesn't help. They tell you to watch for the "warning signs" and all that, but I guess sometimes there really aren't any. Or maybe it's just that we have no idea what they look like. I just want to see and know and understand better is all I'm saying. I don't want to walk through this world without knowing and seeing anymore. I think this has something somewhere to do with past tense but now I am wanting it to be more in the present and that's why I wanted to tell you about my little talk with Morningstar Jackson one afternoon. I think maybe I'm beginning to see things better because of her, or maybe I just appreciate someone who seems like she can see everything.

It was a late afternoon on one of those days and Chuck and I were doing nothing in particular when I guiltily wished that Chuck had an air conditioner, which is of course very unfair on my part because it's not Chuck's fault that he was born in a particular year some decades back. I mean, I was too and I get hot all the time in the summers, who doesn't? Chuck pulled into the shade of the railroad station as I had come to think of it, the willows and the picnic table, and I got out. I wasn't sure why I was here, but that's sort of the problem everyone has, now isn't it? I mean, if you stop and let yourself think about it, which we hardly ever do.

I sat there under the willow, thinking my thoughts, or maybe I didn't because I'm unclear as to whether or not that was a time when I had thoughts. That probably doesn't make much sense so I'll say instead of a much longer explanation that I had somewhere in the past, pretty sure it was then, discovered that it was actually possible to not think about anything at all. Honest. You can do it if you're so inclined. Me, I'm a slope.

Anyway, I happened to be sitting there, looking up at the willow for whatever reasons, the big, big tree that arched over my little table, and maybe I'd seen a bird or something, and so I didn't notice at first that Morningstar Jackson was pedaling in my direction. When I saw her and she saw that I'd seen her, she pedaled fast and then skidded to a stop. I think she does that because she wants a dramatic entrance or something. Truth be told, she probably doesn't need that. I'm pretty sure she's going to just shock a whole bunch of people when she leaves our little town and looks back-ward, maybe just once or twice, and then forward to that big life out there.

"Hi Al," she said, putting down her kickstand, dis-mounting and parking herself on the other side of the table, almost all at once somehow. How does one even do that?

"Hey. How's it going? Where's Thor?"

She grimaced a bit.

"Dentist's appointment over in Helena. Had to take the whole day off from school just to go there."

"Ooo," I said. "Want me to tell you about when I got my wisdom teeth pulled out? Because you know, that's when I got stupid or something, or maybe when I learned the wisdom of hoping to avoid dentist's of-fices. Hard to say."

She smiled a bit, and also grimaced a bit, and once again, how can anyone do that? But she settled in and looked thoughtful and so I asked what was on her mind.

"College," she said.

Okay then. This was something I actually knew a bit about and so I was prepared to mentor her a little on the subject, or at least provide some tidbits of prior ex-perience in one way or another, and at least perhaps be able to play the adult for a change with Morningstar in attendance.

"Are you nervous at all about it? I mean, you shouldn't be. It's fun and exciting and you get to learn all kinds of new things and meet all kinds of new people."

She looked up at me, then down and the picnic table, and then up at the willow.

"No, that's not it. I mean I think college should be pretty good, and I already have half my course work done in the pre-med track."

"You'll be an MD then, or surgeon or researcher?" I asked.

"MD or surgeon," she said.

"So, sounds like you've got it all laid out in front of you. How will it go?"

"Well, that's just it. I have it all figured out except one part of it. I only have two more years of classes, at Harvard, and that's fine and I'm looking forward to them of course and it'll be fun to go somewhere new and everything, and then I have residency after that and have already been accepted to Boston General if my grades are good, and I think they should be. But it's everything after that."

While my head swirled a little bit about someone who was as intelligent and driven as Morningstar, I could only wonder what in the world she could still be concerned about.

"I guess I don't follow you. What's your concern about after your residency? Anywhere in the country, or world, would be happy to have you."

"That's just it," she said with some real feeling. "I don't want to be anywhere in the world or country, I want to be here, in Dobbins, because we have nothing! There's nothing here to take care of people who need to be taken care of and I'm going to do it!"

That sounded very good to me, so I said "Wow. I never imagined you'd be coming back to our little one-horse town. That's great! We really need to have our own doctor."

Morningstar looked at the wind, the wind, the invisible thing that we all know about and cannot see, but I think she does.

"No," she said and stood up and paced around the picnic table while I swiveled as best I could to watch.

"No no no no no. I want more. I want a regional hospital here and EMTs and ambulances and everything. Those stupid friends of yours, throwing themselves down a mountain every year! Then they get hauled off somewhere and I'm not having it anymore! I'm tired of that! I'm tired of what I hear about people getting sick and they'd rather stay in their homes instead of getting taken away all the way to Helena or Missoula. That won't happen anymore. And then they just die and they didn't have to, you know? They didn't have to. That can't happen anymore. And everything else! You even break a finger around here and it's 'Oh well' better put some tape on that and see how it goes'", and she was just stamping around the table now, if one can do that in sneakers, shouting at the sky.

"And if you're a *woman!*" and now she was getting really worked up, "then heaven help you because medicine is about a hundred years behind there!"

And then she wound down, just a little bit. "And I'm taking care of my own parents for sure," she said as she marched around the table, "and we can take better care of everyone else here too. We deserve it! We all work forever just to live here!"

Then she just shouted at the air the wind the weeping willow the wind, reckoning it and measuring it and defying it, and ran around in a couple of circles and came back to the table and put her hands palm-down and looked at me from the other side.

"You're the only one I can talk to! Mom and Dad think I'm 'foolish' and tell me to see what comes, especially Mom. 'Don't dream like that. Wait to see what comes.' She's kind of wired into fate or maybe legends or something, but I see what's coming. I see what I want" and Morningstar thunked her head down on the picnic table, quite dramatically I thought.

She looked up with a stricken expression, something I hadn't seen before, and said "I didn't mean that about Mom. She's been great, so has Dad."

She sat back down, somewhat sliding herself into a form of resolution.

Did you know that when you most want to sit back and ponder something that there's just no way to do so on a picnic table? Sorry, but you just can't do it. You can either sit there, hunch-backed most of the time, or you can somehow straighten yourself, but no. No way you can somehow find a physical way to lean back and ponder what you must.

I opted to lean forward, and spoke softly, a gentle stage-aside voice to this unfolding drama. Maybe that would tell me the missing parts that my brain needed to figure this out.

I leaned forward and said "Okay. I get that. But what has that got to do with college and such?"

Morningstar looked left, right, maybe at the wind, the wind the invisible force.

"You have to understand that I have this all figured you know?"

I simply nodded at that. Of course she did. I mean, really, of course she did.

"The hospital I want, I can maybe do it on my own, maybe, but I need Thor. I want Thor. Do you see? Between him and me we can do anything, we can accomplish anything! Our folks have the biggest ranches anywhere and when we get married then we can do anything and everything! We'll have all the money we want and plenty of people we can employ and all that."

Alright. I sat back on my picnic table bench, and I'm leaving it up to you to figure how I did that. I mean, I kind of had to lean all the way back like in a lounge chair or something to sort of sit back and process all this like I should. I'm not so good processing large chunks of information like I used to. I think we've established that.

Coming out of this revelation, which in itself made me so happy to hear, I couldn't help wonder about things, stories and things, and how they go. Stories go the way they always go, you know, just this way or that, kind of like your own life, you know? So, some stories I know, some of them, they don't work out the way you expect. You're thinking "romance" or "comedy" and then you find out it's something else. You just find out. It's life, you see, and you don't know what sort of story you're in or how it will end up. You never know.

So, I asked.

"Um, but what about Thor? I mean, you know what I mean. You have everything figured out but maybe, you know, but maybe he's kind of a weak link in the chain so to speak? I mean, what does he say?"

Morningstar looked out at the new day, Goddess of Dawn, reflected a moment is all and then turned back to the table across from which I sat waiting.

"I told him he has seven years to put his house in order, because that's when I'll finish up." She looked at me then. "That's from a Shakespeare play I read, that whole 'house in order' thing. You probably knew that. But I told him he could see other girls and like that."

"You did? What did he say?"

"He didn't say anything. He looked me in the eyes like he was sad. I told him he could see other girls and go out and everything." She looked down at her tennis shoes a bit. "I told him that he could, but that I wouldn't. I told him that he'd have to be careful about that."

"Yes. I imagine so. Thor will be a handsome man in his day."

Morningstar looked at me again, a bit of a frown scuffed her forehead. "Yes he will. I know. And so I told him that. I told him he'd have to be careful because in seven years I was going to come back and he'd be mine. I told him. And then we could be together and do whatever we want."

"And what did he say?"

Morningstar looked away, and then down, and then up at the willow. The breeze blew just this way and that, ruffling the leaves.

"He said, he said that he would wait. He said that if I really promised, that if I really promised, he would wait. He said that if I came back, that I really promised to come back, then he could be happy forever."

We sat there just a little bit longer, looking at the birds, the trees, the leaves, the wind, something.

"Did you make that promise then?"

"Of course I did!" she cried, like I was completely stupid.

"Of course I did," she said again, looking at me as if I might deny it.

I let out a breath I didn't know I'd been holding.

"Yes, he will. He'll be waiting for you, I know he will. You'll come home at Christmas and spring break and maybe just a week or two between terms in the summer, right?"

She nodded. She almost cried. But she smiled instead.

Afterward, I had to think about it. You see, I absolutely trust everything that Morningstar says. I know you don't know her like I do, but listen, if she puts her mind to something, anything at all, then you'd better believe it's coming true. That's just the way it is. She has a plan and it's going to get done and that's all there is to it. She has a plan. She's thought it through.

I needed to start thinking again.

CHAPTER THIRTY-SEVEN:
A FEW THOUGHTS ABOUT GIL

I ended up writing a piece in The Paper about Gil. It was a lengthy piece, but Chip and Jeff were okay with that. During the week some people had gotten together and taken his sled down to the Good Gas along with the trophy and put it up so people could see it. That just made my stomach turn, but nobody besides me and Walter and Jeff and Chip knew what that sled had meant, and we weren't going to ever tell anyone.

I wrote about the Good Gas of course, but I wrote about its history and why it had come into being in the first place and how Gil had given up his other plans of being a paleontologist, archaeologist, and anthropologist, and had decided that he had better stay in Dobbins. It hurt me to write these things, but I wanted to say something, even in just a back-handed way, about what he had really wanted, and what he had sacrificed, and what he had loved.

Chip and Jeff told me that now it would become the McMasters Memorial Run forever after, and we stood around for a bit looking at the floor and then we cried.

And what I wished I could have said, what I wished I could have shouted, simply, to anyone, was that Gil was deeply unhappy and we none of us ever knew it.

We none of us saw it coming. You're told to see the signs or something; you're told to be watchful. We didn't watch. We didn't see.

CHAPTER THIRTY-EIGHT:
THE BOOT IS ON THE FENCEPOST

The majority of the people who live in our enormous county, which is roughly the size of several of those states that are part of the original colonies all combined, don't happen to live in Dobbins. Most of us live out on some parcel of land, small or large, because that's either where we want to be or that's where we have to be. As a result of this, quite a lot of us don't have a home anywhere near what you'd call a "main road" of some sort.

Ranchers, for example, usually have their homes way the heck out somewhere that's centrally located on their spread because that's the logical thing to do, and consequently, a lot of people's "driveways" might be miles long or more. The reason I'm telling you this is because you have to understand why it is that when you're driving along someplace and you see an old boot on a fence post next to a dirt road headed off somewhere that this means something to people around here. It means the home owner is actually home. No boot on the fence post and that means you can save yourself the drive out to somebody's place because nobody's there.

Kenna later told me that it was a maybe two weeks after Hollis and I met up that she came home and saw two pretty chewed up boots on the gate posts to their place. Instead of driving on up her driveway, which is maybe a mere fifty feet of rocked lane, she parked her car and got out and looked at the boots. There was one on each post, left and right, and she thought she recognized them. They were in pretty bad shape. They'd certainly never be worn again by anyone in their right mind.

Then she looked down and saw blood on the rock. There was quite a bit of it in fact, and as she slowly went up the driveway she could see that the bloody marks continued, at an even pace mostly, all the way to the front door. When she reached the porch, she saw two very large and very distinct footprints outlined in blood.

Like I say, Kenna only told me this later on, but even then she was swearing and mad and just about to chew nails in half, and she said she stood on the porch for a while until she cussed herself out and then opened the door without bothering to try her key because she knew it was unlocked. She came inside and there in the front room lying on the couch with his feet up on the coffee table on a dish towel was Hollis, dead asleep.

She saw the bloody footprints leading to the kitchen and then back to the couch, and she didn't say a word. She got closer and saw that Hollis' feet were absolutely raw and bloodied and ruined. Hollis stayed asleep. Kenna looked at his feet again and put her hand to her mouth, and then she got a chair and pulled up and sat down opposite of him and looked at him for awhile. If his boots were in pretty sad shape, then Hollis himself was no better.

After a while of sitting there, shaking her head, she went out to the back room where they kept their doctoring things like we all do, and came back with creams and ointments and gauze and scissors and she sat down. She pulled her chair up to his feet and with a cloth and bowl of hot water she washed as much of the clotted blood away as she could.

This whole doctoring of him was difficult because she couldn't easily see what was a wound and what was a bruise, but she did her best. She got up once to get the tweezers because she saw she was going to have to pull quite a bit of whatever it was out of his wounds. There were rocks. Splinters. Maybe even asphalt had joined itself to them. She did what she could. Then she rinsed them, cleansing the very deep wounds no skin could cover. Hollis slept on.

That worried her all of a sudden and she looked up and saw his chest rising with his breath. Yes, still alive she said to herself.

Finally after having removed what she could from his feet, she took the ointments and creams and gently tried to swab them on, and then lightly wrap on the gauze, and that was the best she could do. She got up and went to the dresser in the bedroom and got out a pair of winter's boot socks, big as she could find, and then came back and slowly put them on his feet, one at a time.

She returned to her chair and looked at him, worry deepening her look.

Hollis opened one eye.

"That was amazing," he said with just a tiny whisper of a voice. "I love you. I have to sleep."

Kenna cried a bit and swore a little bit, and Hollis slept a dreamless sleep. She went and made herself some dinner.

CHAPTER THIRTY-NINE:
YOU NEVER KNOW

Somewhere sometime I was, and I wish I could say where and when but those little details have been erased I think because they didn't matter, don't matter, never did, and I was someplace sometime sitting somewhere and felt a thing, a flutter in the breeze or a movement in time, or perhaps something in my not-looking-right-at-it vision, it's hard to say, but it made me look up. Whatever it was I was doing I looked up. You never know.

I think I was at that picnic table by the old railroad station that doesn't exist anymore, that old crossroads that doesn't cross any roads any longer, that place where no one comes but me. I think that was it, but it doesn't really matter.

I think the willow branches hung down like strings of Mardis Gras necklaces, saying something about penance and beginnings; I think they hung down just like weeping willows always do. I think they hung down with new leaves, because willows are always the earliest. I think the trees were old. I think they were there long before Dobbins. I think they leafed out without you knowing that they did. You can't just watch and see you know. You can never be always watching and seeing. You never really know for sure just when they do.

And so they leaf out. And one day you see when the day before you didn't.

She parked her truck and got out. She had no long-rider coat from winter. She had no hat. She had an eye-patch. Her hair was on one side but not the other. She was the pirate of everyone's dreams, striding her way down the deck to give the day's orders. She was the one-eyed Raven. She was this world right now and all the others. I stood. For just a bit I stood there because I was afraid the light might change, the breeze might shift, something, and then I would be seeing something else from somewhere and sometime else. But it didn't, it didn't, and I walked forward and we smiled and hugged. I stood back and she stood back and we looked around at nothing and everything.

"The willows are just now leafing out," I said.

"Al, it's been over three weeks now."

"Really?"

I hadn't noticed.

We sat and talked but I don't remember what we said. It all had the sound of new leaves and whatever it was they always say to one another and whatever it was it was all green and new.

CHAPTER FORTY:
THE PRESENT TENSE

Chuck is taking us home. I am having a moment, a short period, of lucidity, perhaps like someone in a hospital, waking from something else, just briefly remembering a thing. It is a problem for me, this rousing to remember.

I remember.

I remember Joanie and I as kids, still in our teens and twenties, back in Washington, each of us with a fly rod in hand and wading down the Skykomish, each of us on opposite banks and trying different stretches of the river, and we'd wave to one another and point to some place to meet up again, not being able to speak to one another against the roar of the river, moving with the currents, taking us each just this way and that, meeting up again at the confluence of two branches in the river somehow always not so far ahead.

I remember once when we were backpacking that somehow we got separated and one of us went off on a different trail for miles and miles and had to backtrack, and then exhausted after coming back, there at the signpost, hours later, was a note that said "This way!"

I remember another time when we went camping next to a river, and it rained like mad and we kept hearing these strange sounds in the night, like something jumping into the river, but we didn't get out to look in the dark and the rain. When we got up the next morning we saw a landslide had passed us in the night, and new boulders were near our tent. We were fine. We laughed.

I remember when I got my first teaching job and Joanie was so happy for me and so proud of me and said we should have something special for dinner and we had pizza even though we couldn't afford it.

I remember our first cat, who we snuck into our apartment, and later our first dog, and did the same thing even though she was a German Shepherd. We laughed so much about that.

I remember us sitting in the Jeep, with the top off, staring at the skies while we rested in the dark on a mountaintop in Washington, and we weren't tired even though we'd been driving all day just to get there. Who could be? The stars were so close you could reach up and touch them, and they rained down on us later as we put a blanket over ourselves in the cold mountain air.

I remember making a bookcase from planks and cinder blocks and Joanie saying she didn't think that was going to be big enough.

I remember surprising Joanie one night after I had picked her up from work, and I wore a dress shirt and tie and we came back to the apartment where I had dragged the table out into the front room and surrounded it with our plants, and served her our first shrimp vindaloo in candlelight.

I remember being so sick that I couldn't see straight

and slept twenty hours each day, for almost a week, and Joanie brought me soup and dry bread, because we couldn't afford a doctor, but she made me live again.

I remember once, I cannot say when, but something terrible happened, beyond what you'd ever imagined, and then there was home, and embraces, and the smell of one another's hair.

I am remembering not remembering. It has a taste like stale air. I lean over and roll down the other window because Chuck is driving and I am trying to remember. I am present tense. I am sure. The air gushes in and I want to just lean back in it: good, hot, summer air, just blasting me in the face. It is so good.

There are just a couple of hours left for me to put my house in order, not much more than that. If I really am in the present tense, then I must understand that this is all that's left. This is all there is.

Chuck drives on and I begin to doubt where I am. I may not make it in time. If I get there, and find out that I've completely misunderstood, that I didn't know *then* and this had all taken place a long time before and I was now just forgetting everything all over again, and everything was once again meaningless, then I guess I would finally see it, and know it for what had happened. And that would truly be the end.

But I was still almost sure I was in the present tense. Almost certain.

Chuck drove on, and I believe we were headed north again, going home, but I really didn't know. Past present future. There were mountains, and we were going up and then down them, and then we came to a pass and dropped down into Dobbins, good ol' Dobbins, and it was summer I saw, just glorious summer all over again. Amazing! I was right!

We came through town and I waved at everyone I saw. If Chuck had had a horn I'd have beeped at everyone too. I had made it. I'd made it back to the present.

When Chuck pulled us up the driveway and I'd gotten out, and then walked into the house and found no one was there, I walked out back and there was Joanie, sitting in a chair, reading a book in the sunlight and Grip and Tan were asleep in the grass at her feet.

"Hi," I said, and Joanie was surprised to see me.

"You're back early, what happened?"

"Oh, nothing really. I guess I just got a little bored is all."

Joanie looked at me for a minute and said "You got bored? You got bored of fishing? You okay?"

"Yeah, I guess so," I said. "Hey, remember the vaudeville show down in Silver City we're always hearing about? Everybody says it's really funny, you know? Well, I got us a couple of tickets for Friday, and I stopped over at Delmer's and he said he and Dorothy could feed the dogs that evening and make sure they had some exercise."

"You got tickets to that show? How'd you get tickets?"

"Like I said, I got bored so I drove down there and got them. It's just a couple of hours from here is all. So, what d' you think? Want to go? It's supposed to be very good."

"That sounds good," Joanie said.

Later, now I'm sure it was later, on the drive down to Silver City we talked about puppies, and that maybe we should get one soon. Joanie said she'd been thinking about that too. It made us feel good to think about a puppy. Joanie said she'd already been looking into it, doing some research. I was glad.

Later, on the drive back home we had to rub our faces to get them to work again. We'd laughed so hard and for so long at the show that our faces were sort of locked into a permanent laugh. We had never laughed so much in our lives. We laughed all the way back home too. We re-told some bits from the show and laughed and laughed again and said "No! Don't say it again! I can't laugh anymore! My face hurts," and I just about drove off a straight-as-an arrow highway because I was laughing so much I could barely see.

Still later, yes, I know it was later but I don't remember just where and when, there was a puppy and I held him in my arms and put my face into his fur and it smelled like smoke after he had come inside with Tan and Grip from the cold, cold night. And I remember the smell of Joanie's hair as well. Everything just seemed all a-fire right then.

CHAPTER FORTY-ONE:
WHAT I REMEMBER IS FISHING

Past present future, I don't know. Everything is scrambled somehow and it's hard to know. I want to use the word "remember" but I don't know if that's the right word. You can change things in your mind you know. You can make them different or pick out a detail that was once minor and make it everything, and you can erase things that you don't want to think about. You can do whatever it is you want to in your mind.

What I remember is fishing. We were standing in a long drift, him above, me down below. I was below because the run was narrower, and he took up above because he had pity on me because he was far and away the better caster. We stood in the snow-melt water, white and furious wrapping itself around us, and it was another glorious morning on the river, and everything was alive in every brilliant detail.

In front of me was the river. It was white blue black yellow and the colors that cannot be said as the morning descended down the canyon. He was up above I remember, and I was down below. I remember. I cast into what was white and it turned to blue and then out into the golden molten sunlight of dawn and my tiny fly, this thing of no consequence to anyone or anything, was somehow gone, and I didn't understand right away, but I think I remember. I am trying to remember what it was.

I had never yet hooked a Steelhead here on The River, and when my line jolted and my rod bent then I called out to him and even above the roar of life that galloped past us, and beyond his own reckonings and imaginings and daydreams and calculations, he pulled himself from the current, doggedly wading against it, no master of his, and then he made his down the boulder-strewn passage and was by my side.

We stood, and I stood, we are past present future now because it is The River you see, and we're all of us caught up in it wherever you are, but for us we're in it in the now, and he is behind me and says what he says and I lift my rod and he says again what I should do and he says yes and no and I trust him and I lift my rod because the end is in sight. I see it. The fish will catch the current, the current that can't be held back by something as insignificant as your line.

When the fish jumped, a scene of silver chain-mail in the drafts of sunlight and shook the hook, a temporary tether to our own lives, I stood in the water, its life rushing around me, and finally breathed again. We stood on the bank, and he told me how it goes. He was so happy for the loss, the fight, the glory of *almost*. I didn't understand. I can never understand.

What I remember is fishing, but it wasn't, it wasn't fishing like I want to remember because we were sitting there in the office two days before he died, two days before the killer came, and he was telling me about how he had this one guy in class who he knew was going to be a problem and he told me a bit about it and we said what we said about those sorts of students. And then that was all. And this of course was the killer, the mass murderer, and we were talking about him, briefly, and grimacing while we spoke of such students of the past.

I have this in my mind past present and someone's future. I have tried not thinking about it. I cannot stop thinking about it.

If you say these things to anyone then they will say that you couldn't have known you couldn't have seen you couldn't have understood. And yet I want to have known, I want to have seen, and I want to have understood, but that is all past tense. And I worry about the future.

THE END

www.ingramcontent.com/pod-product-compliance
Lightning Source LLC
Chambersburg PA
CBHW061506120726
48001CB00004B/1233